The Harmonics of Love

Corinne Arbeau

WHISTLING
RABBIT
PRESS

San Diego, California

The Harmonics of Love

by Corinne Arbeau

Copyright © 2017 Corinne Arbeau

Published by

Whistling Rabbit Press
San Diego, California
whistlingrabbitpress.com
Contact the publishers at info@whistlingrabbitpress.com

Interior design by
Deepak Gupta @fiverr.com/weformat
Contact the designer at guptadeepak2353@gmail.com

Paperback ISBN: 978-0-9847360-6-5

eBook ISBN: 978-0-9847360-2-7

For music lovers

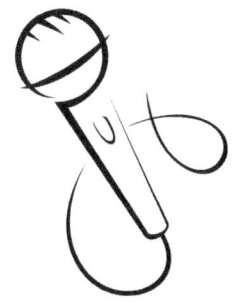

The Harmonics of Love

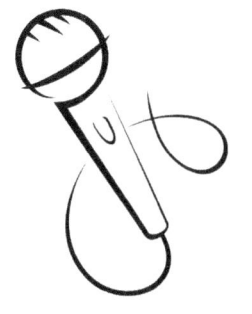 # CHAPTER ONE

The night Uncle Teddy came to have dinner with Catlyn and her parents, he seemed different—slightly electrified and louder than usual, if that was possible for a boisterous guy. Catlyn suspected something was on his mind. Sure enough, after the dinner dishes had been cleared away and her parents were out of the room, he turned to her.

"Cate, I've got an opportunity for you," he said, his bushy eyebrows raised. Only he pronounced it "opportunité," like it was French. Uncle Teddy didn't look very sophisticated, with his down-home clothes, worn boots, and big gut, but Catlyn had learned that he was a man of surprises. Nevertheless, she really didn't think he spoke French.

"An opportunité?" she mimicked him, raising her own eyebrows back at him. "Coming from you, that sounds very suspicious."

"Hear me out," he said, putting up a large hand. "It's for the Pitchforks." The Pitchforks, also known by their full name as the Rusty Pitchforks, were Uncle Teddy's band. Teddy played lead guitar, flatpick mostly, and he was backed by a handful of the ugliest guys to ever squat on a stage—large, hairy, fleshy guys whose hands could turn remarkably deft when handling a fiddle, mandolin or drumstick.

"The 'Forks?" Catlyn said. "What are you guys gonna do, rob a bank?"

"No," said Uncle Teddy. "We have a new singer, and he wants a backup singer."

"Oh, Uncle Teddy," said Catlyn. "I'm too old." When she was little, she used to sing with the Pitchforks on some of their bluegrass tunes, a kid in pigtails that everyone declared "so cute." Now that she was 18, she cringed at the thought of standing in front of people with her mouth wide open like a dork.

"You are not!" said Uncle Teddy. "Was Emmylou Harris too old when she sang behind Gram Parsons?" Catlyn rolled her eyes. Sure, she could sing a little, but she was no Emmylou Harris, that was for sure.

"Come over on Thursday," Uncle Teddy said. "Just check it out. You might be surprised. The 'Forks are taking a new direction." He chortled. "Hey, I like that. Like a new 'fork' in the road." Catlyn rolled her eyes again.

Nevertheless, on Thursday, after work at the coffee shop, she changed her clothes to head over to Uncle Teddy's. The band practiced on Thursdays and Sundays in his garage, a tight, airless box, but it was the biggest space any of the band members had available, and one where the noise of the band wouldn't bother the neighbors. People would pay to hear live music, but having to listen to a band practice would bring out complaints faster than somebody cutting in the beer line.

The thing was the Rusty Pitchforks were good. They played a lot of covers—country, bluegrass, old-timey music, even some rock 'n' roll—but they had an original sound, musically complex but with a good beat that everyone could tap their feet to. Much of that sound came from Teddy whose wide fingers on a guitar could spin some amazing intricate tales, but the guys behind him were talented too. Tall skinny Woody played the fiddle, and Catlyn recalled how she used to remember his name because he looked like a tree, swaying this way and that, as the notes poured out of his instrument. Bo was their utility infielder, playing bass, rhythm guitar, sometimes a mandolin, and rarely a banjo—to the groans of the other band members. Another big guy, Bo's size belied his alert eyes and ability to move in behind a wandering jam and lasso it back on course. The center of the rhythm was Grommet, a hulking bear of a man, who sat behind his drum set barely moving but never missing a beat. His drum set—if that's what you want to call an array of drums, beat makers, bells, weird pipes, odd percussive tools—took up half the band's space and provided the heartbeat of the band.

Catlyn was thinking about the Pitchforks as she got dressed. They were all like uncles to her; Teddy really was her uncle, her mother's brother, but Woody had been with the band when she sang with them as a kid. Grommet came later but long enough ago that she didn't remember when. Bo was "new"; she remembered him joining some years ago after Mac Brown's diabetes got bad and he couldn't play anymore. She knew Uncle Teddy was in his fifties, but she had no idea about the rest of them. They had that timeless look of older guys with beards. They could be anywhere between forty and seventy, she thought.

She pulled her hair back in a ponytail and chose a yellow summer dress and sandals. The dress wasn't new, but it looked all right, and it was a change from Catlyn's usual outfit of jeans and boots. She wasn't dressing up exactly, but she didn't want to look like a slob either. Her mother gave her an approving look when she walked into the kitchen for a glass of water.

"You look nice," Marie said. "You're not going to be cold?" The days had been getting warmer, but it was still early May and evenings were chilly.

"It gets hot in that garage," Catlyn said and wrinkled her nose.

Her mother nodded and called out to Catlyn's father in his office, "Robert, are you driving Cate to Teddy's?"

"I'm ready when she is," he called back. Catlyn's family had two road vehicles—her dad's truck and her mother's Ford hatchback—but between the three of them, there weren't enough cars to go around. They lived five miles outside of town, and it seemed like one car or another was always on the road. Robert came into the kitchen, his tall frame filling the doorway. He was still a good-looking guy in his mid-forties, lean and clean-cut, a contrast to the Pitchforks. Catlyn's mother joined him in the doorway, her head only coming up to his shoulder, but no slouch in the looks department herself, still pretty and fit.

"I'm going to stay at Uncle Teddy's tonight," Catlyn told her mother. "I'm working at the Cuppa Joe again tomorrow, but I'll be home for feeding." Catlyn's parents raised chickens and a few beef cattle along with their food crops, and it was Catlyn's job to keep the animals fed and watered.

"You got your stuff?" her mother asked, and Catlyn held up a bag with a change of clothes. Marie gave her a kiss, and Catlyn and her dad went out the door.

"Thanks for driving me," Catlyn said to Robert during the drive.

"My pleasure," he said and gave her a smile. "It's not every day I get to drive a star."

Catlyn smiled back but said nothing. She wondered how he knew about her being invited to sing with the band. It's not like it was a big deal. Everyone knew the Pitchforks were good, really good for a town like Upton, but Catlyn was old enough to know that there were lots of good bands in the world, and she had no illusions about the prospects of some old guys who could pick a little. Besides, she was just helping Uncle Teddy out; she knew being a real singer wasn't in her future.

"Look, deer," said her father and chuckled. Catlyn spotted the doe and fawn by the edge of the road, heads thrown up high, startled by the truck. They stood like frozen sentinels as the truck barreled past, and the last rays of the sun shone through their ears. Catlyn thought of the quiet that would return to the road after they had passed, after the engine noise faded away and the dust settled, when the deer would return to eating. She knew that stillness; she had spent many hours in this countryside and on this road. She knew its bird calls, the whirr of a grasshopper, a fish plopping in the creek, a cow's faraway moo. *The countryside's lullaby; Everyone knows their part; We'll sing together by and by; We've learned it all by heart,* she rhymed in her mind. Nature made a different kind of music, but one that came as naturally to her as her own heartbeat.

"Here she is!" sang out Uncle Teddy when Catlyn came into the kitchen. He was stirring up some iced tea, from a Lipton mix, Catlyn noticed with a shudder. How could he drink that stuff, she wondered, when sun tea was so easy to make and so much better.

"Go on out," he said. "Morley's already out there."

Catlyn made her way through the mudroom, navigating past rubber boots, recycling bins, hanging overalls and fishing poles leaning in the corner, to reach the garage. When she stepped inside, her eyes went immediately to the young man who was fiddling with a microphone at the front of the garage. She was struck by how young he was, almost as young as she was, but his self-confidence was evident, his back straight and his movements animated. He peered at the switch and wiggled the cord.

"What the hell…" he muttered.

He had curly brown hair, a little too girly for this part of the country, but his muscular arms, well-developed chest, and slim hips would have made him a looker anywhere. He wasn't tall, maybe just under six feet, but he seemed to draw the eye, as though a spotlight were on him. He was dressed in jeans and sneakers, and his clothes hung on him as though he were a model in a fashion magazine. She suddenly realized Bo and Grommet were grinning at her, amused at how she was checking out the new guy.

"Hey, do you know where—" Morley turned and then spotted her.

"Hi," he said, smiling slightly, and cocked his head at her.

"Cate. Morley," said Bo by way of introduction. "He's from California."

"Pleased to meet you," said Morley and bounded over to shake her hand. Catlyn thought he hadn't really *bounded* over, but that was the word that came to mind. He seemed full of energy, and it conjured up an image of Tigger from Winnie the Pooh and his bounces. His hand was surprisingly warm in hers and sent a wave of heat up her arm. She shook awkwardly, unaccustomed to shaking hands, but Morley gave her hand a firm squeeze.

"You're from California?" she asked, confused by the boy, the handshake, the light on his hair. *It looks almost golden*, she thought distractedly. *Why is it lit up like that?*

"Yeah, by way of Austin," he said and smiled directly at her.

Friendly, cute, nice teeth, really cute—wait, Austin? her poor brain prattled at her.

"Austin, Texas?" she said, struggling to appear normal.

"Yep," he said and turned back toward the guys with a question about the microphone.

Catlyn put her bag and purse down in a corner, trying to process the appearance of this golden boy in her uncle's dingy garage. To say he looked out of place would be the understatement of the decade. And what was someone from Austin doing *here*? Catlyn knew enough to know that singers from Austin would not join the Rusty Pitchforks.

Something else was different too. The garage looked as though it had been straightened up, nothing extreme, but paint cans were put away, tools hung back up on nails, some old tires missing. And the garage had been swept, maybe the first time Catlyn remembered ever seeing it tidied up. And another thing was different. The guys were hanging around quietly by their instruments, tuning up or adjusting things, not messing with each other and drinking beer like they usually did at rehearsal. Catlyn had been at Teddy's house often enough at rehearsal times to know that beer was the musical lubricant of choice.

On cue, Uncle Teddy appeared with the iced tea and handed glasses all around. Catlyn declined, knowing what lay in store, but the rest of the band took swigs and made appreciative noises, setting the glasses carefully down on the floor. Morley also took a glass and took a sip while Catlyn surreptitiously kept an eye on him. When the sugary, tangy, artificial drink hit his tastebuds, Morley grimaced. And right then, Catlyn decided he was a jerk. Who was he to waltz into her town, shaking people's hands, and making faces over iced tea? Uncle Teddy had been very kind to make up a pitcher for everyone. Fine, if Morley—what kind of name was that anyway?—liked the iced tea in California—or wherever it was he was from—he could just go straight back there and drink till he choked.

Having resolved this issue in her mind, Catlyn was not prepared for what happened next. After some discussion, the band had laid out a song list, some standard country tunes, an old bluegrass number, and a Hank Williams song.

"We'll figure out the rest as we go along," said Uncle Teddy.

"Chime in whenever you feel comfortable," he called over to Catlyn who was standing off to the side in front of a microphone that loomed large in front of her face. When she'd tested the microphone, she was so quiet that the guys thought at first it wasn't turned on. Now, it appeared to be threatening her as though it intended to jump down her throat. She stood miserably, unhappy to be there and still aggravated at the rude intruder.

Her heart leapt however when the band started up. They began with *Joe's Place*, a contemporary song with an old-fashioned theme. It was a favorite of Catlyn's, but when Morley began to sing, it was as though she had never heard the words before. His voice was strong, deeper than you'd expect for his size, but layered and rich, full of timbre and resonance. He was never off-key, but he played with the pitch and rhythm, creating an emotional backdrop to the simple melody like Catlyn had never heard before. *He sings like Frank Sinatra,* she thought suddenly. She was so mesmerized by his voice, she stood dumbfounded, and only thought to join in on the chorus near the end. The moment her voice came through the speaker, louder than she expected, she saw his back tighten, and she knew he had heard her. This so unnerved her that she fell silent again all the way through the rest of the song. When the song was finished, he turned and gave her a little nod. For some reason, that made her mad too. Who was he to be nodding at her like some bandleader? This was Uncle Teddy's band, which she had been a part of—even if it was a long time ago—not him.

Nevertheless, she stayed quiet for the next song, unsure of what to do. Besides, it was hard to sing along when that voice was charming its way through the words, clipping here, drawing out there, each line a mastery of technique. Catlyn knew the difficulty that went into making singing look that easy and sound that good. His voice is really warm, she thought, it's like when the sun comes out from behind the clouds. *His sweet and roaming tongue, Spread around the sun, Like honey on a bun,* she rhymed and then stopped, startled by her own thoughts.

"How 'bout *Pink Houses,*" Morley suggested, and the band kicked into the Mellencamp classic after a few false starts. Catlyn knew the song well. Like most local teenagers, she'd sung along many times while it blasted out of some car radio. But she was still intimidated by that damn microphone, and let a chorus go by without a peep. To her embarrassment, when the first chorus finished, Morley turned to her and made a "what-the-heck" gesture, his hands open at his sides. It was both an invitation and a challenge that he followed up with an arched eyebrow before he turned back to his microphone for the next verse. When the chorus rolled around again, Catlyn screwed up her courage, opened her mouth, and sang. It wasn't smooth; it wasn't notable, but it did put a female voice behind Morley's deep tones. Even Catlyn heard right away what a good addition it was, and Uncle Teddy gave her an approving smile. Catlyn managed some backing woo-woos and lit into the next chorus with more enthusiasm. She'd show him, that snotty Californian-Texan, whatever he was. Carried along by the music, she sang through the chorus and then forgot that the final line went to the lead singer. To her horror, she heard herself over the speaker, while the rest of the band went silent, stomping on Morley's final line. For a brief moment, she hoped that it would go unnoticed until she saw Morley tense and turn toward her. The song ended, and the guys busied themselves with their instruments. Morley stared at her.

"Excuse me?" he said aggressively and stared at her wide-eyed. Catlyn's face turned hot, and she looked at her feet. Uncle Teddy stirred, but Morley put a hand out toward him.

"This will only happen once," he said to him. Then, to Catlyn, "That's my line."

"I know," she said. "I'm sorry."

"That's not good enough," Morley snapped. "Don't do it again." Then he picked up the song list.

"Okay, what's next?" he said as though nothing had happened.

I hate him, thought Catlyn. *He's arrogant and rude. Uptight,* she concluded. *Typical Hollywood prima donna.* She decided that she would never sing backup for him again. Uncle Teddy could just find someone else to do it. Good luck with that in this town.

Morley's attention to detail however made the band better. He and Uncle Teddy went through the songs before and after each was played, and made comments and notations on the chord charts of improvements and embellishments they wanted to include. Grommet had a laser focus on the beat, and Catlyn had never heard the band sound so tight. And Woody was playing like there was no tomorrow; his fiddle sang and wailed like a live animal.

Despite her anger, Catlyn became caught up in the songs spooling out of the band. They played *Honky Tonkin'*, and Morley's sexy interpretation was good enough to get on the radio, she thought. When he sang a Johnny Cash song, chills went up her back. She joined in with enthusiasm, and to her surprise, Morley gave her a grin.

Sooner than she expected, it was over, and the guys were packing up their instruments and trading ideas for next time. Morley and Uncle Teddy began discussing the next rehearsal, and Morley called out, "Sunday work for everybody?"

Affirmative grunts came from Bo and the others, but Catlyn said nothing. As far as she was concerned, *never* would work for her. Morley said something in a low voice to Uncle Teddy, and he mumbled back. Catlyn didn't hear what they said, but she was pretty sure they were talking about her. She gathered her belongings and decided to bluff her way through the discussion.

"See you guys later," she called out loudly and stepped out of the garage into the mudroom.

"Nice to meet you," Morley called back, and then, "Wear something else next time. You look like a banana."

Catlyn's instant rage at his impertinence was only a tiny bit lessened by the implication that he expected her to return. She was further enraged by what she thought was the sound of the other guys snickering. She heard Uncle Teddy say something, and then Morley protested, "It's for her own good. She—" But Catlyn didn't wait to hear anymore. She slammed out of the house and then realized that she wasn't leaving. She slammed back into the house and strode to the little bedroom that she used when she stayed in town. She shut the door hard, flung herself on her bed, and stewed.

After everyone had left, Uncle Teddy rapped on her door.

"You okay, Cate?" he asked. "You need anything?"

"No, I'm fine," she lied, deciding to pretend that she wasn't upset.

"Okay," he said and wandered away. Catlyn heard him messing around on the guitar a while later. When she had calmed down, she picked up the writing paper she kept at Uncle Teddy's and began scribbling.

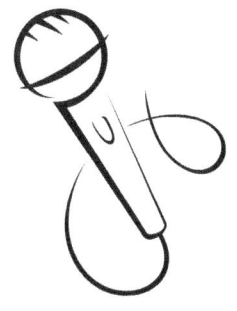 CHAPTER TWO

The next day, she walked to the Cuppa Joe to open up with Sherice at eight a.m. The Cuppa was the town's only coffee shop, an oasis of charm in the otherwise no-frills town. Sherice managed it and tried to create an ambiance with what little money she could spend on aesthetics. Catlyn helped out at the shop five days a week, and Sherice paid her what she could. They had known each other since third grade and without needing to say so, were best friends. Since it was Friday, she and Catlyn had lots to do to prepare for the weekend, stocking and baking pastries, and cleaning the coffee jugs. It was after noon before they took a break and nibbled on some leftovers. Catlyn needed someone to commiserate with so she told Sherice about the rehearsal and about the new guy.

"Is he cute?" Sherice asked immediately. Sherice had a live-in boyfriend, but that didn't keep her from checking out the goods, so to speak.

"He's got the looks, all right," said Catlyn. "And an ego to go along with them."

"Aw, dang it," said Sherice. "Isn't it always like that? Can't guys ever be nice *and* good-looking?" She sighed. "Want to go outside for a cigarette?" Catlyn didn't smoke, but she kept Sherice company during her smoke breaks when she could. Sometimes she thought she just enjoyed the vicarious bad-girl thrill. Through the smoke, she told Sherice what Morley had said about her dress.

"How rude!" said Sherice, just as she was supposed to. Then, "What were you wearing?"

When she heard about the yellow dress, she pressed her lips together. "Cate, you do know what country singers wear, right?"

Catlyn protested, "I'm not a country singer, and—" She was going to say that she was not about to start dressing like those singers on television, but Sherice broke in.

"How 'bout you and I make a trip to the thrift store?" she said. And before Catlyn processed what had happened, she had agreed to meet Sherice on Saturday to look for a new outfit. She wasn't sure why she was agreeing when she had no intention of going to the Sunday rehearsal, though shopping with Sherice was always fun. Sherice gave her a lift home, and the two speculated about what a California boy would be doing in town.

"Maybe he's on the run from the police," Sherice said.

"Yeah, the etiquette police," Catlyn groused.

"Everything okay with you and Danny?" she asked delicately. Ever since Sherice's boyfriend had smacked her across the mouth a few months back, Catlyn worried about her, but the bruises had faded and the incident appeared to have passed.

"Yeah," sighed Sherice. "He knows I'd kill him if he tried anything again."

On Saturday, Sherice and Catlyn found a red silk blouse at the thrift store that would go okay over some jeans and a trim leather skirt that showed more of Catlyn's legs than she was comfortable with, but Sherice talked her into it.

"What's the point of looking like you do, if you never show it off?" she said, looking at Catlyn in the mirror. She tweaked a lock of Catlyn's long blond hair. "And promise me, you'll wear this down, for once, okay?"

Somehow Saturday passed without Catlyn calling Uncle Teddy to announce that she wouldn't be there on Sunday. And so she found herself, dressed in the new blouse, jeans, and boots, driving herself to Uncle Teddy's in Robert's truck, early Sunday evening. She hummed the chorus of *Pink Houses* before she caught herself and turned on the radio.

As she walked through the mudroom, she heard voices from the garage.

"I'm not saying she doesn't have potential," she heard in Morley's deep voice. "Hell, if you tell me she has potential, I believe it. It's just that—"

Uncle Teddy interrupted, "I want you to give her a chance."

Catlyn knew from Uncle Teddy's tone he had made up his mind. When Uncle Teddy took that tone, no one in the band argued with him. Apparently, Morley hadn't gotten that memo because he started again, "She doesn't—"

But Catlyn would not learn what Morley thought she didn't because, just then, she walked through the door, and he fell silent. Both he and Uncle Teddy made a show of busying themselves with the equipment after they said hello, and an awkward silence fell while the rest of the guys arrived and set up their instruments.

Catlyn was mulling over the conversation she had overheard and had forgotten about her new blouse until Woody turned to her and said meaningfully, "You look very nice today."

"Actually, yeah," Morley turned and gestured at her. "That looks good." Catlyn could hardly believe her ears or her eyes, either, as Morley appeared to be slightly disconcerted. For once in his life, he looked— dare she think it—uncomfortable. Regardless, she had no sympathy for him. He had waltzed into her town, had embarrassed and then insulted her, and argued with her beloved uncle. He had a lot to make up for.

Uncle Teddy spoke. "I'd like to start with Cate singing something for us," he said simply. Catlyn could have hugged him. What a gracious and considerate way to start the rehearsal. And then it dawned on her that he meant for her to sing by herself, effectively a solo. She nearly staggered with fright. Sing all by herself with that—that *Californian* listening? She turned toward Uncle Teddy in distress, but he barely glanced at her.

"How about *Gunpowder and Lead*?" he said. "You know that one, don't you?"

She did know that one, the girl-power anthem by Miranda Lambert. With as much airplay it had gotten around here, you'd have to be deaf not to have memorized most of the lyrics. Catlyn had liked the story of the song too, so she had learned it by heart. How did Uncle Teddy know that? Had he heard her bawling out the song in the shower? Suddenly, Catlyn was sick of it all, the questions, the insecurity, the doubts—not only from Morley, but from herself.

"Fine," she snapped and whirled on Morley. "You sit over there," she ordered and pointed at a chair in the corner of the garage, out of her line of sight. "Ready, go," she said to the band, and the guys scrambled to start the intro and set the beat.

Catlyn was fired up, and she addressed the microphone as though it was Morley's face and she intended to get a few things straight. When she heard her voice come over the speakers, however, she almost lost her nerve. She was determined not to back down now, but she felt terribly alone, trying to carry the melody by herself. She saw Grommet pause slightly, to slow down and give her a moment to collect herself. Woody was standing by, his kind eyes on her, ready to follow her lead. Uncle Teddy picked a riff to set up her next move. What was it he used to say to her? From so long ago, she remembered.

"Don't think about how it's you singing," he had said. "It's someone else's song, and you want to respect that. You're just the messenger." It *was* someone else's song too. Catlyn could never be that tough girl in the song waiting for her abusive husband to get out of jail and show up at home where she planned to welcome him with a shotgun. But Catlyn remembered the flash of white fury that had shot through her when she had seen the nasty black and blue marks on Sherice's face, and how she had wanted to find Danny and teach him a lesson. Maybe using a shotgun to assist in that teaching moment wouldn't have been such a bad idea.

Catlyn started in on the song, and the band locked in behind her. She focussed on the words, on the story, and forgot about her uncertainty of the last few days and her hurt and irritation at that damn handsome man behind her. Her voice came out sure and determined, as she set the stage for the chorus. She knew the backstory of the song too, how Lambert had been inspired to write it, after an abused wife and her child had come to stay in Lambert's parents' house. Catlyn practically spat as she dove into the chorus, Uncle Teddy filling in the color. Grommet set a pounding beat, and Catlyn found the words flying out of her, until she finished the last chorus, and the band brought it home with a raucous cheer. As the guys hammed up their finale, Catlyn found herself grinning. She cut her eyes slightly to the right to see the reaction of the Californian. Morley was sitting down, as he had been directed, but just barely. He was perched on the edge of his chair, like he was about to spring up, with his hands on his knees, staring at her. And—how delicious—it looked like his mouth was open. *Take that, sonny boy*, she thought, and then almost immediately, *That's a really good name for him.*

It turned out that was that. Morley stood up and was all business, conferring with Uncle Teddy about what songs he wanted to bring Catlyn in on. They added some backup parts for Catlyn to *Sunshine and Whiskey* and *Room to Breathe*. Despite their difference in age, Morley and Uncle Teddy seemed have the same musical mind. They hardly used words when they were figuring out where to go with a song. One would snap his fingers or hum a little, and the other would jump in. They made cryptic notes on their music sheets, but it seemed to Catlyn that when they played, those scribbles turned to magic in the air.

"How about *American Saturday Night?*" asked Morley, and the band fumbled around to get the bass line and beat going. Once Morley launched into the first verse, however, they were swinging, and Morley rocked in front of the microphone. Catlyn loved the song, its good-time vibe, and clever lyrics. She joined in on the chorus as soon as she could and provided enthusiastic whoo-woos during the bridge. Uncle Teddy went nuts on the guitar solo, and Woody's fingers were flying on the fretboard. When the band closed it down with a big finish, Morley cackled.

"That's a keeper," he said and added, with a sly look at Catlyn, "She likes Brad Paisley. Why am I not surprised?"

Catlyn lifted her chin at him. "I like that song," she corrected.

But the mood was high in the garage that afternoon. The band was coming together, and everyone knew it. Practice was set for Thursdays and Sundays from 6 to 8 p.m. which worked in the guys' work schedules since they all had day jobs. Grommet owned a plumbing business, Bo did handyman work, Woody didn't work full-time now, but he still did carpentry, and Uncle Teddy—well, sometimes it was hard to know what Uncle Teddy did. He was an insurance broker for nearly everyone in town, but it seemed like people came to him for all kinds of legal advice or paperwork. For the band, he kept the administrative side of things organized. This afternoon, he got them to put everyone else's phone numbers into their phones.

"Not sure I've ever had a guy give me his niece's phone number before," said Morley and winked at Catlyn.

"You be careful with that," warned Uncle Teddy.

"Hey, Cate," Morley said to her. "I can spend some time with you on Thursday, after rehearsal, to go over some stuff." She looked at him and considered. After the session in the hot garage, he looked a little disheveled and sweaty. *Kind of sexy*, she thought and then, embarrassed, looked away. He hesitated.

"Just if you want," he added. Catlyn caught herself. Of course. It was a nice offer.

"Yeah, thanks," she stumbled. She glanced up at him. He was taller than she was, but not by a lot. *Just the right amount*, she thought and winced. He gazed at her, puzzled.

"Sure. See you then," she said quickly and rushed out of the garage.

On Thursday, the band put in the effort and worked up several more songs, including *Drinkin' Problem* and *Giddy-Up and Go*, one of Uncle Teddy's originals that was maybe about horse racing and maybe about sex. The way Morley sang it, Catlyn was pretty sure that it was about sex.

She paused when the two hours were up, unsure if Morley's offer still stood. He glanced over.

"You gonna hang around for a minute?"

She nodded. The guys seemed to be hurrying to get out of there, but Morley came over and started messing with her microphone.

"I think that might be a little better for you," he said, lowering it a bit.

"Stand here." he put his hand on her waist and moved her in front of the microphone and looked at where it reached on her. He showed her how to stand back from the microphone and move in when she sang. He explained how she should sing close to the microphone except when she was projecting. Then she should pull back to make the volume more predictable for the audience. He demonstrated coming in soft and ending soft, so that there were no abrupt changes in volume. Catlyn listened carefully and took it all in. It *was* very helpful.

He also gave her some tips about what to do with her body—in a professional way.

"A lot of backup singers just stand there. I guess some lead singers don't like it if the backup singers move around, but I like it. It adds energy to the stage. Plus it keeps you more relaxed. So try something like this," he stepped behind the microphone and showed her some moves.

"Now, you try it," he said. Catlyn tried to do what he had done, but she felt stiff and self-conscious.

"It's okay," he said. "It'll be easier when there's music. Just remember you're the only girl in the band, and you're easy on the eyes, so people are going to be looking at you. You have to keep your eyes on me so we stay together, but that doesn't mean you can't be doing something a little bit interesting."

"That's why I said that about your dress the other day," he added, without the slightest sign of remorse. "People will be thinking about what you're wearing, so you want to play the part." Catlyn wasn't sure what he meant by that, and she was still distracted by the "easy on the eyes" bit, but she figured she could ask Sherice what "playing the part" meant.

"Now, here's the thing," Morley went on, more serious now. "I can't sing every song. Teddy's talking about doing three fifty-minute sets. I'll die, or my voice will die, even if he takes a few numbers. And the rest of these guys sound like frogs farting. So, you're going to have to sing some solos—" He raised his hand as Catlyn started to speak.

"You can do it. *I heard you*," he said in aggravation as she shook her head.

"Here," he said. "I've put down a couple of songs that I think you would do really well. Check these out, work 'em up, and we'll see what they sound like on Sunday."

Catlyn looked down at the fragment of paper he handed her. He had scrawled *I Feel Lucky* and *Born to Fly* on it. The first was one she knew from the radio, a funny, saucy song by Mary Chapin Carpenter.

The other was a Sara Evans song, but she was less familiar with that one. She stared at the paper. It dawned on her that Morley had gone to the effort to think about songs for her.

"I—"

"Get them ready for Sunday, and I'll have the guys work them in," Morley said.

Catlyn looked up at him.

"Thanks," she managed to say.

"Well," he said. "Don't thank me yet."

He had a point. On Sunday, when Uncle Teddy announced that the band was ready for *I Feel Lucky*, Catlyn lit into it with enthusiasm. It was a fun song, and the band sounded great. She sang all the way through while Morley watched from his assigned corner—without being told this time. The guys hooted when she concluded, but Morley held up his hand. He pointed out that she had come in on the wrong beat in the second verse, had forgotten one of the spoken lines, and had substituted the word *to* for the word *for*. Catlyn felt happiness ebb out of her as he spoke.

"Who cares," she muttered about the word substitution.

"Hey," said Morley intensely. "There will be a girl in the audience who sings that song every day on her way to work. She knows the words by heart. She cares that you get them right. And you should too."

They went through the song again, with Morley stopping the band each time he had a correction to make. They reworked the spoken lines, the problems with the rhythm, and Catlyn's growl. He had her growl over and over into the microphone until he deemed it a success, long past the time she felt like an idiot.

"Yeah!" He fist-pumped when she had executed the perfect growl. The band stayed alert and patient during all the minutia. When Uncle Teddy called for a break, Morley walked over to Catlyn.

"You're doing great," he said and leaned in toward her ear. "It's just a process, you know, right?"

She nodded, but she was nervous about *Born to Fly*. It was one thing to slam bang your way through boisterous songs like *Gunpowder and Lead* and *I Feel Lucky*. *Born to Fly* was an inspirational song and required more finesse.

Morley squeezed the back of her neck and patted her shoulder. Catlyn noticed Uncle Teddy glancing over at them. She wasn't used to Morley's casual touching, but it seemed to come easily to him. Truth be told, his hands were warm and reassuring, and she didn't mind how they felt.

The song went better than she expected. The band helped a lot, and Morley showed her some ways to make notes of the melody easier to reach. After some practice, she began to really enjoy the song, how it soared and did really make her want to fly.

"I knew that would work for you," said Morley.

CHAPTER THREE

The band was continuing to bring in songs and muddle around with what would work in their sets. They had added some fiddle tunes, a Charley Pride number, and a couple more originals. After some hesitation, Catlyn screwed up her nerve and suggested *Silver Thunderbird*, a song she thought was well-written, and played it for them on her phone. They agreed to try it out, and Uncle Teddy went to get the music sheets. Morley frowned when he looked over the lyrics, but he executed the vocals with the kind of craftsmanship she expected.

"I get it!" he said after the first run through. "It's about a car." He grinned at her.

After a little more practice, the Pitchforks declared that one a good addition.

Uncle Teddy updated the band on their prospects for playing in public. The Rusty Pitchforks used to be the house band for The Corral, the big roadhouse up the highway that entertained a diverse crowd on weekends. The owner was getting antsy while the 'Forks were undergoing their new "direction" because business had fallen off. He had booked a few bands, but none could draw the way the Pitchforks did.

"We're looking at the first Saturday in June," Teddy said. "There'll be a photographer here on Sunday for the promo poster, so bring your best duds."

Morley spoke up. "I get it that he needs to bring in some money," he said. "But we shouldn't take a gig if we're not ready." Uncle Teddy shot him a look.

"Then, let's make sure we're ready," he said. Morley might be a perfectionist, but some of the guys relied on the gig money.

On Sunday, under orders from Sherice, Catlyn wore her leather skirt for the photo session. Morley whistled when she walked into the garage, and the guys all turned to look. Catlyn felt her face go pink, but they stumbled over themselves to say how good she looked. Morley smacked her on the butt when he got the chance.

"Foxy lady!" he exclaimed.

"Hey! Sexual harassment," she protested but couldn't help laughing.

"Oh boys, I'm in trouble," Morley clowned. "Better give me a smack on the wrist." He held his hand out to Bo who instead slapped his palm approvingly.

"Ow," said Catlyn, rubbing her behind in a pretense of pain.

"Calm down, everybody, it's just a skirt," said Uncle Teddy, but he was smiling.

At the Cuppa the following week, Sherice showed her the poster that had arrived to be put in the window. "The Rusty Pitchforks, featuring Morley," it announced. Catlyn looked closer at the poster. Her leather skirt seemed to be a couple inches shorter than she remembered, appearing more like a mini skirt than a normal skirt. And had they done something to her boobs? They didn't look right. Sherice shared none of her concerns and announced that she looked totally hot in the poster.

The next two weeks passed in a blur of rehearsals, work at the coffee shop, and chores at the farm. Planting season had arrived, and Catlyn helped with household jobs while her dad spent most the day out in the fields or working on the equipment. So far, the weather was cooperating, and her parents were tired in the evening but optimistic about the upcoming season. It sometimes seemed to Catlyn that farming was either dealing with something that had gone wrong or waiting until it did. *The farmer starts each year with fresh hope*, she penned one night. *Works the field to a slippery slope; Always has on hand just enough rope.*

Opening night finally arrived, and on Saturday afternoon, Catlyn helped Uncle Teddy pack up the stage monitors, microphones, amps, and sound equipment into the back of his truck. The roadhouse could provide stage equipment, but Uncle Teddy always said he'd rather stand on a golf course in a lightning storm than rely on the Corral to keep the band from being electrocuted.

The Corral was a good fifteen miles out of town, so the band usually tried to share rides. Uncle Teddy and Catlyn stopped by Mrs. Scales' house to pick up Morley. Catlyn knew that Morley was living in Mrs. Scales' basement, but she hadn't been there before. Uncle Teddy sent her in to tell Morley they were outside. She pushed open the screen door and called out, "Knock knock."

"Down here," she heard Morley yell from down a flight of stairs by the door. When she arrived at the bottom, she saw Morley standing by an unmade bed on the other side of the basement. A set of weights was stuck in a corner, and a refrigerator and hot plate were arranged under a bare lightbulb. The place struck her as dismal until Morley turned toward her. His pants were undone, and he was tucking in a shirt. He had on a dark jacket, and the light struck him across the face, highlighting his cheekbones and lips. He smiled when he saw her.

"My, my," he said. Catlyn was wearing the famous leather skirt but had also curled her hair and put on a little makeup, as directed by Sherice. In addition, she was wearing some cowboy boots that Sherice had insisted she borrow. She blushed as Morley appraised her.

"Now," he said. "You have to be my mirror. Do I look okay?" She looked him over, at a complete loss for words. How could she tell

Morley that he drew the light in the basement like a new sun, causing the dank walls, washer and dryer, broken shelves and single lightbulb to fade to nothing, leaving illuminated only this vision of a handsome man fastening his jeans?

"You look fine," she said and started back up the stairs.

The other guys were already at the Corral and unpacking when Catlyn, Morley, and Uncle Teddy brought in their first load of stuff from the truck. Uncle Teddy sighed.

"Gotta face the music," he said and headed toward the front.

"Face the music?" Morley said, confused. "Do we have to face the music?" he asked the other guys.

"No, moron," said Bo. "You are the music."

Donelle, who handled the bookings for the roadhouse, such as they were, stopped by to see if they had what they needed.

"Y'all sober?" she asked.

"Temporarily," said Woody.

"Good," she said. Looking Catlyn over, she said, "You are as pretty as your poster, honey. I ain't seen you in years."

"Thanks," said Catlyn shyly.

"Listen, if you don't want to hang out with these jackasses during the break, you just come find me, and I'll give you a pop." Then she caught sight of Morley.

"Oh," she said. She seemed struck speechless, and Catlyn wanted to giggle.

"Hey, where are our M&M's with the brown ones picked out?" said Bo.

Donelle swatted him on the arm.

"Actually, I only eat the brown ones," said Woody.

"Well, then, you'll be fine as soon as you find the bag," Donelle said tartly and walked out.

"I'll take my chablis now," Bo called after her. Then he turned to Catlyn. "Is chablis a thing?"

Uncle Teddy was gone a good ten minutes. When he returned, he put up a finger and waved it in front of the whole band, like a mini windshield wiper.

"If anyone asks, she's twenty-one," he said. They stared at him and then turned in unison and stared at Catlyn. She stared back. It had never occurred to her that her age was a problem.

Morley walked over and put an around her waist. "This old bag?" he said.

"I thought she was twenty-two," said Woody.

"Me too," said Bo. "Or older even."

"Hell, I thought she was older than me," Grommet put in.

"I'm just more mature," said Catlyn. They all hooted at that.

As they moved to the stage to set up their equipment, they continued to give each other a hard time. Catlyn floated around in a fog of happy bliss. Their opening night was finally here, and she was overjoyed to be part of the band. She couldn't wait to show the crowd what a night they had prepared for them. After they were introduced, the guys stood aside so Catlyn could walk out onto the stage first.

"Send her out first," said Bo. "In case they throw something."

A huge cheer went up from the crowd when the band walked out. The house lights were still up, but the stage lights hit Catlyn in the eye, momentarily blinding her. Then she could see there were people on the dance floor already, and it looked as though the bar was busy too. As she took her place behind her microphone, she looked out at the crowd—what she could see of it at least—beyond the flood lights. They looked up expectantly, and she beamed back at them. She was filled with anticipation and exhilaration. Morley must have shared her feeling because he bounded to the front of the stage and threw his arms open to practically embrace the crowd.

"Good evening!" he called. He looked sharp, dressed in the jacket that contrasted dramatically with his golden hair under the bright lights.

The crowd called back with a mixture of good evening, yo, how ya' doin', and cheers.

"Let's get to it!" Morley shouted, and the crowd yelled its approval. Uncle Teddy's guitar rang out the opening notes of *American Saturday Night*. The band kicked in, the house lights went down, and the crowd roared all in quick succession. Morley grabbed the microphone out of its holder and danced across the stage during the intro, turning to grin at her, before he whirled to deliver the opening lines. His voice coated the crowd with its deep resonance and melodic overtones, the speakers doing justice to the layers of complexity in his delivery. He was confident, sexy, and mesmerizing. Catlyn noticed some girls at the bar, staring at him as though he had just fallen out of a spaceship. But she couldn't think about that because suddenly she was swung into the chorus, and the band was rocking, Grommet driving the beat, and Woody's fiddle sending cascades of notes spiraling up to the ceiling.

The first set flew by. The crowd cheered appreciatively when she sang *I Feel Lucky*, especially when she growled. Morley whooped and got the crowd to give her a big hand. At the break there wasn't much time for talk, just enough to gulp down some water and do a quick review of the upcoming songs. Sherice stopped by for a minute to say hi. Her face was pink with excitement. Danny was over 21, and he must have snuck Sherice in somehow. She told Catlyn she was doing great and looked fabulous, mostly because of the boots.

"And you were right," she whispered. "He's *so* hot."

"Sherice!" Catlyn elbowed her and then gazed happily at her friend. There was no one else like Sherice, and she gave her a hug. Then she had to get back to work.

Morley touched her shoulder and said that they would do *Born to Fly* near the end of the set. This was good for Catlyn since she was so engrossed in keeping up with the band that she didn't have time to get nervous. She was almost surprised when she heard the first drum notes of her song and Grommet glanced over at her. Fired up by the band, she felt ready—more than ready—gave him a big smile, and started in. When she got to the part about the brown-eyed boy, Morley jerked a thumb at his chest and wiggled his eyebrows at her hopefully, making the crowd laugh. Someone in the back gave a long wolf whistle. Then they were into the chorus, and Morley was singing with abandon, head thrown back, eyes closed, hand on his chest, his voice soaring with hers. She could see how the cords of his neck stood out above his collar, and even from behind him, she could feel his power and his passion, the joy that he took in singing about this girl *with potential* who was born to fly!

His energy was contagious, and standing with him, she too felt filled with inspiration. The crowd was clearly taken with him too. They ogled him from the floor, their faces turned up expectantly. They watched, or howled, or danced with their hands in the air. For his part, Morley put his all into serenading them; he coaxed and wooed each of them, looking directly into their eyes. It was as though he was sending a personal message to every heart in the place. There were lines that he delivered so well that people crossing the floor stopped in their tracks and stared at him open-mouthed. They even paid attention when he introduced the band. Catlyn looked out at her people, thunderstruck by this singer, having such a great time, and she couldn't stop smiling.

When the third set was over, the band tumbled into the backstage area, sweaty and full of adrenalin. They were still milling around in exhilaration when Donelle showed up with a tray full of Michelob and a pop for Catlyn.

"Beer in a bottle," said Bo. "What will they think of next?"

The guys clinked bottles, and everyone drank deeply.

"Hell of a night," said Morley, almost to himself, and then turned to Catlyn. She braced herself. She knew she had flubbed a couple lines and had almost came in at the wrong time on several choruses. She'd only caught herself by reading Morley's body language. Somehow his shoulders had a way of signaling when it was her turn. She was surprised when he raised his bottle to her.

"You rocked," he said, "for a blue hair."

"To the blue hair," repeated Woody and gave her a toast. A rush of pleasure passed through her, interrupted by a knock on the door. Bo went to go see who it was and was back in a minute.

"It's for you, lover boy," he said to Morley. Morley set down his beer and went to the door. Everyone stared at Bo.

"Some girls," he said by way of explanation. "They, ah, looked pretty hot to trot."

"Dang," he added after a minute. "Now we have groupies."

"Strictly speaking," said Woody. "*Morley* has groupies."

No one besides Catlyn seemed surprised at this turn of events, and the guys set about packing up their stuff. Morley didn't come back, and his beer sat condensing on a stool.

"Ready, Cate?" said Uncle Teddy, once they had gotten the equipment loaded into the truck.

"What about Morley?" she asked dumbly.

"Morley's a big boy," said Uncle Teddy, looking amused. "He can take care of himself." Catlyn was embarrassed and went to the truck and slammed the door. *Singers can just come and go,* she thought to herself. *Do re mi **fine** la ti do.* They rode in silence.

"You did a good job tonight," said Uncle Teddy. "I'm proud of you, Cate."

"Thanks," she said, and for a second, she felt better. It had been a fabulous evening. She just hadn't expected it to end like that.

CHAPTER FOUR

Morley showed up for rehearsal the next day like nothing had happened. Catlyn looked for clues that he was hung over or had spent the night carousing or doing something else she didn't want to think about, but he seemed as insufferably cheerful as ever. Something unusual did happen during practice though. Morley and Uncle Teddy were talking about how they needed more traditional dance numbers in their set list. The crowd at The Corral clearly liked to dance, and the Pitchforks had the chops to make them happy.

"How about *Why Don't We Just Dance*?" Catlyn offered, unable to restrain herself. She loved the song and could already hear Morley's deep voice sweet-talking his girlfriend into turning off the television and cutting a rug. She played a sample on her phone, and Grommet started drumming along.

"I like it," said Morley and gave her thumbs up. Woody caught on to the fiddle part right away, and in thirty minutes, the band was playing the song like they'd been working on it for weeks. Catlyn had been right. Morley's delivery was perfect—inviting, amusing, and oh so sexy. When Uncle Teddy and then Woody took a solo, Morley waltzed over to where Catlyn was standing behind her microphone and held his hand out. Catlyn stared at him in alarm. Was he asking her to dance with him in front of the band?

"Come on," he urged and pulled her to him. She stumbled, but he caught her and then pushed her around with his hand on her waist. She managed to execute an awkward twirl under his hand. He grinned at her and headed back to the microphone to finish the vocal.

"That's a good idea," he complimented himself. "Just needs work. Can you stay after?" he called to Catlyn.

"I guess so," she said, too surprised to say no. She glanced at Uncle Teddy, but his face was hidden. So, that's how she found herself "practicing"—that would be dancing—with Morley after the rest of the band had gone home. He showed her how to step out from behind the microphone and move into his arms and then bounce back for the two-step. He took her hand to position it below his shoulder so she could feel his motion and follow along. She tried not to be distracted by the definition of his muscles under his shirt but couldn't help noticing how sure and graceful he was in leading her around the floor. *The boy can move*, she thought. *He's in a groove.* They practiced the right-hand turn and a promenade until she could follow easily. Morley turned some music on and danced her around the garage with some new moves thrown in for spice.

"The crowd's gonna love this," he said happily when they had gotten pretty smooth. "How 'bout you?" he asked. "You enjoying yourself?" Catlyn had to admit that she was. Dancing with Morley was fun, and she noted ruefully that *of course* he was a good dancer. After he spun her around the floor a few more times, he bent his head toward her ear and asked, "Are you ever going to invite me to your room?" She almost panicked.

"Let me re-phrase that," he said when he saw her frozen face. "I mean, can I see it? Because I want to." She almost laughed, her discomfort with his activities of the previous night forgotten. He was still holding her hand, so she led him to the little room off the living room and opened the door. The house was quiet. Uncle Teddy must have gone out.

"You don't have much stuff," he said in surprise, looking around at the spare room furnished with a cot and a dresser. The closet door was open, and a few clothes were hanging on hangers. A poster of Jerry Garcia hung on the wall.

"This isn't my regular bedroom," she said, finally understanding. "This is Uncle Teddy's spare room. I just use it when I stay in town."

"Where's your regular bedroom?"

"At my parents' house outside of town."

"Huh," he said, "is that where you keep your stuffed animals?"

She narrowed her eyes and glared at him, although, in fact, she did have stuffed animals in her bedroom at home. She had to resist the urge to stick her tongue out at him. He just smiled at her and picked up Uncle Teddy's old six-string that Catlyn sometimes fooled around on. He sat down on the cot and began noodling out some notes. He tuned a couple of strings that were out of tune and gave her a look.

"I don't really play," she said defensively.

"Nor do I," he said. "Nor do I."

But as if to contradict his statement, he began strumming and then eased into *Don't Think Twice It's All Right*. Catlyn sat down on the floor to listen. His singing was straightforward without some of the vibrant overtones she could hear when he was miked. But it had a sweetness to it that was lost in the roadhouse amplification. It was his guitar playing that surprised her most however. His fretting hand moved easily and surely up and down the neck, and the fingers on his picking hand moved like spider's legs to fill her room with melody. It was lovely, and Catlyn was spellbound until the last notes were through.

"I didn't know you could play," she burst out.

"Ah," he said, "there's playing and there's playing. I can't hold a candle to your uncle."

"Sure," she said, "but you're no slouch. How come you don't play with the band?"

"I'm the singer," he said.

"But lots of singers play guitar," she protested.

"Not this one," he said. Then he added, "To me it's a distraction— just something between me and the audience."

She thought this over. It was true that when Morley sang, he gave the impression that whatever distance there was between him and the crowd, he wished he could shrink it. He shimmied and lunged and sang *to* them. He engages them, she thought. I've never seen a singer do that. It's like he wants to make love to them—Morley interrupted her thoughts.

"Besides, nobody ever watched Elvis play guitar." He plucked a couple notes and then hit a few harmonics on the neck. *Ding Ding Ding.* Catlyn adored those sounds. Uncle Teddy played them sometimes.

"What are those?" she asked.

"These?" He played them again. *Ding Ding Ding.* "They're harmonics."

"How do you do that?" she asked.

"Come up here, and I'll explain it to you." Morley patted the seat next to him. Catlyn joined him on the cot, and he gave her the guitar. With his fingers guiding hers, he showed her what frets harmonics can be played on and how to hold her finger lightly over the string to produce the high-pitched sweet ringing note.

"How does it work?" she asked.

"Your finger is dividing the string in two, so you're making what they call a new node," he explained. "Now the string is vibrating between the nut and the new node and the bridge." He pointed to the top and bottom of the neck.

"Oh, so the string is making a new sound," she said. "That's why it's so high."

"Actually, the sound is always there. You're just deadening some of the overtones so you can hear it better."

"Like getting rid of a distraction."

"Exactly."

"They're so pretty."

"Like a lot of things when you look closer."

She turned to look at him, but he yawned and leaned back on his elbows on the bed, bumping into some of Catlyn's notebooks.

"What are these?" he said.

"Nothing," she said, hurrying to set them on the floor. He was quiet for a moment and then sprang up.

"Want to get some air?" He took the guitar from her and reached out a hand to help her up. She was surprised at how easily he pulled her up. She could see his bicep flex under his sleeve.

"It's late," she said, glancing at the clock. It was after ten, and she worked early the next morning.

"I won't keep you out long," he promised.

Catlyn closed the front door behind them, and they headed down the walkway to the street. The street was empty and quiet. Lights were on in the houses they passed, along with an occasional television set. Catlyn put her head back to look at the sky. There was no moon, and stars shone, far away. *Pin pricks in my cocoon*, she thought, *sailing through the giant blaze of our galaxy*. They walked in silence for a while. Cate was determined to keep her cool in front of this gorgeous boy who seemed to fluster her at every turn.

"Is Cate short for Catherine?" Morley asked.

"No," Catlyn said. "My name is Catlyn."

"Wait," Morley said. "K-a-t-e—uh, l-i—"

"No, c-a-t-l-y-n," said Catlyn.

"Y?" said Morley. "There's a y in there?"

"C-a-t-l-y—" began Catlyn again and then giggled. "I'll write it down for you."

"Wait, I can get this," said Morley. "C-a-t-l? Y? Why? Why is there a Y? Then N?"

"That's it," said Catlyn.

"There's no Cate in there at all," said Morley outraged. "It's Cat-lyn."

"What can I tell you," said Catlyn. "According to you, my name is misspelled." She giggled again.

"I'm gonna call you Cat," said Morley. And easy as pie, he reached out and took her hand and swung it a little. "I guess that explains why you go from zero to sixty in about two seconds."

"What do you mean?" said Catlyn. His hand felt so warm in hers. *Cozy*, she thought.

"You know how you can be tickling a cat's tummy, and she seems to like it, and then, all of a sudden, wham, she's stuck her claws in you."

"Hmm," said Catlyn. She wasn't sure she liked the analogy and decided to think about it later. "What about your name?" she asked. "Where does Morley come from?"

"Moreland. Moreland Graham, at your service," he said, with a little bow.

"Moreland, how do you spell that?" said Catlyn. "M-o-r-l—"

"No, m-o-r-e-land," said Morley.

"But you spell it Morley m-o-r-l, with no e," said Catlyn.

"Guess my name's misspelled too," said Morley and cocked his head at her.

"Where does it come from?" said Catlyn. "Moreland, I mean. I've never heard it before."

"My mother dreamed that one up," said Morley. He didn't sound very happy about it. He dropped her hand and put his in his pocket. "You wanna head back?" he asked and turned without waiting for her answer. *So much for that,* thought Catlyn.

She wanted to ask more questions, about his mother, and what his life had been like, but the mood had shifted, and he didn't seem to be open to any more questions. They walked back toward the house.

After a few minutes, he spoke again. His voice sounded brighter. "I don't think I've ever been on a spelling-bee walk with a girl before," he said, and she could sense him smiling in the dark.

"I just like words," Catlyn said.

"I know," he said and took her hand again.

"I can think up some harder ones," she offered.

"I'll bet you can."

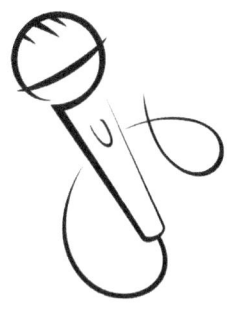

CHAPTER FIVE

Sherice and Darryl and some other friends from high school had sent texts around saying they should go out to the lake on Thursday. Catlyn said she couldn't go until after the Pitchforks' rehearsal was over, and they said they'd wait for her. Darryl texted he was driving, and his truck was in the driveway when rehearsal wrapped up. Sherice came in to the garage to say they were waiting outside. Catlyn introduced her to Morley, and Sherice looked him up and down with appreciation. Catlyn was embarrassed at her friend's brazenness, but she needn't have worried.

"Hey, you should totally come," Sherice said to him. "We're going out to the lake. It's fun. We make a bonfire and stuff. You can ride with us." Catlyn wondered just how long Sherice had been planning to make this "spontaneous" invitation.

"Thought you'd never ask," Morley said enthusiastically.

Catlyn, Morley, Sherice and Danny all jammed into the back seat of Darry's truck while Darryl's girlfriend, Wendi, sat up front with Darryl. Darryl nodded at Morley when they were introduced, and Wendi said, "Hey, aren't you that guy from the band?"

"Yeah, I'm kind of their roadie," Morley said, and Sherice laughed. Catlyn saw Darryl eyeing him in the rearview mirror; she knew that wouldn't go over well with him. She studied him from the back seat. She and Darryl had hung out when they were in high school. They didn't see each other much now that he had a girlfriend, but she felt as though she could still count on him if she needed help.

"So what's California like?" Sherice was asking Morley.

"Awful," he said.

"No, come on," she protested. "Sand and sun—I would love it there."

"Not where I lived," said Morley. "More like smog and strip malls."

"Where were you at?" asked Danny.

"L.A." said Morley. "The Valley."

"Oh, yeah," said Sherice, playing cool. "I'm, like, from the Valley," she said to Danny.

He guffawed. "Right. Like… my ass," he said. Everyone snickered.

Catlyn hadn't expected to be riding out to the lake with Morley, but she was intrigued that he was coming with her friends. She liked going to the lake—the sand, the moonlight on the water, and the sound the waves made lapping at the shore.

"So how far is it out to this lake?" asked Morley.

"Twenty miles," said Sherice.

"Twenty miles!" said Morley.

"Don't worry; it'll go fast," said Sherice flirtatiously.

"We came prepared," said Danny and held up a six-pack. "Wanna beer, Valley Boy?" he asked.

"My man!" said Morley. "I was starting to think I was in a dry county."

"Nearly," said Sherice. "But we're not quite that backwards."

Morley popped open the beer and took a swig.

"Want one?" he asked Catlyn. She shook her head.

"Cate doesn't drink," said Sherice. "Well, except *sometimes*," she added and raised her eyebrows meaningfully.

"I'd like to hear about *sometimes*," said Morley.

When they got to the lake, there was already a bonfire going, and earlier arrivals were perched on logs pulled up around the fire. Sherice laid out a blanket, and she and Danny arranged themselves on it and lit a joint. There were quite a few people, including some guys who always seemed to show up whenever there was an outing at the lake. Either they live at the lake, Catlyn thought, or they have an app on their phone. *Party at the lake, gonna shake and bake, cool kids on the make,* she rhymed. Somebody had pulled out a bag of chips and was handing it around. Some of the guys had a paddle ball game going, and someone handed Morley a paddle. He had taken his shoes off, she noticed.

"I'm ready," he yelled, hopping around in the dark. "Can't see a thing." He feigned an athletic leaping backhand shot. "Did I hit anything?"

Someone served him the ball, and Catlyn could hear the sound of the ball hitting the paddles and the players' cries as she headed down to the shore.

"Cate."

She turned to see Darryl catching up with her.

"Hey," she said. They walked together.

"So, is he your boyfriend now?" Darryl asked, and it sounded only slightly teasing.

"What? No," she said. "He's just… in the band," she finished.

"Kind of an asshole," Darryl stated.

"He's just… different," she said.

"Lot of different kinds of assholes," Darryl said.

It didn't really surprise her that Darryl would take an immediate dislike to Morley. That kind of cockiness would rub him the wrong way, she knew. Darryl was an old soul; he'd grown up fast when his mom got sick and he'd had to help his dad with the household. In the old days, Catlyn had liked that about Darryl. He was reliable and made her feel safe. Driving out to the lake was an example. He preferred his own driving; it bothered him when kids drank and drove. A while back, some older kids had gotten drunk and wrecked their car on the two-lane highway coming back from the lake, and Darryl had said they were stupid. He might have a beer or two, but he wasn't like the guys who drove out there and got wasted with no thought for the drive back.

Darryl could be judgmental though, with a well-developed sense of right and wrong behind those dark eyes and watchful silence. He wasn't afraid to call people on their crap either. She'd seen him lie in wait for some unsuspecting flake only to strike at the opportune moment. He was likely to get away with it too; he wasn't heavy, but he was tall, at six two, and most people didn't mess with him.

"How're things with Wendi?" she asked after they had walked for a few minutes.

"Good," he said. "We're talking about getting married."

"That's great," she said. "Congratulations."

"Well," he said. "Talking ain't doing."

"Still," she said. It seemed like a big step to her, but kids around here often married young, some right out of high school. That's just how it was.

"How about you?" he said. "You got anybody?"

"No… who'd have me?" she joked.

"Don't say that," he said. "You deserve somebody really special."

She wondered why Darryl hadn't turned out to be her somebody special. She'd liked him a lot. He reminded her of her dad, though maybe not as funny. She wasn't sure why they'd split up; they'd just seemed to spend less time together, and then he had shown up with Wendi.

Back at the bonfire, someone had turned on the radio, and a few kids were dancing in the sand to the B-52's *Love Shack*. Danny and Sherice had vanished, and the guys with the paddleball game, including Morley, were gone too. Catlyn sat down on one of the logs next to a guy named John, who she knew was vaguely related to Bo, a cousin or something. She'd seen him at the roadhouse on Saturday with a date.

"You were great Saturday night!" he greeted her. "The band was awesome. We had a blast."

"I saw you with that good-looking girl," Catlyn said. "That your girlfriend?"

"Nah, she dumped me," said John.

"That didn't take long. Smart girl," said a girl sitting on the other side of him.

"She doesn't know what she's missing," he said.

"That singer's pretty good," said the girl, leaning over to talk to Catlyn. "How old is he anyway?"

"I don't know," said Catlyn.

"Must be in his twenties, right?" she continued. "Wonder what he's doing here. Don't seem like someone like that would hang around here long."

"Yeah, well, shit happens," said Catlyn.

"You got that right, sister," said John.

Later, Catlyn was sitting on the blanket talking to Wendi when she became aware of a ruckus nearby. Just outside of the range of the firelight, she saw two figures who appeared to be engaged in some sort of argument. Suddenly, the taller figure shoved the other, and she could see in the firelight that it was Darryl. The shorter figure paused for a moment and then shoved the other one back. She realized with a thump to her gut that it was Morley. Darryl and Morley were fighting. She leapt to her feet and ran toward them, Wendi on her heels.

"Hey!" she shouted, running up to Darryl. He looked down at her; he was breathing hard.

"He said you were eye candy!" he said outraged. He looked disheveled.

"I did not!" yelled Morley. "I said—I said any band could use some eye candy." He sounded a little drunk.

"Same difference!" argued Darryl.

"Not at all," said Morley, swaying slightly but with irritating smugness. "I was speaking hypothetically."

Catlyn would have laughed except for their evident anger and the continued threat of violence, as the two men stalked around each other. She suspected that they were both drunk, and maybe a lot drunk. Morley laughed suddenly.

"Dude!" he exclaimed. "It's not like it's a bad thing. It's not like I insulted her."

"You shut the fuck up," Darryl yelled back, infuriated, and made a move toward him again. Wendi ran forward and got her arms around him.

"Come on, baby," she said and pulled him away. Catlyn walked up to Morley. He blinked when he saw her.

"Well, that went well," he said brightly, with a slight slur in his voice.

"Let's get out of here," said Catlyn. She asked John if they could hitch a ride with him, and Morley got into the backseat of his Honda while Catlyn went to go find Sherice to tell her they were leaving. When Catlyn climbed into the backseat, she felt a hand slide up her denim skirt, all the way up her leg to her panties.

"Hey!" she exclaimed, so startled that she bumped her head on the ceiling. But when she looked at Morley, he was looking out the window apparently innocent, with his hand in his lap. Had she imagined the hand? But she could still feel the tingle and caress of that warm flesh. She looked at Morley again suspiciously.

"I like your friends," he said conversationally. Catlyn couldn't resist laughing. In fact, once she started, she couldn't stop giggling.

"You are a piece of work," she said to him.

"That's a good thing, right?" he said.

The next day, Sherice showed up late to work, but she was animated when she did.

"What the hell happened last night?" she said, her eyes wide. "Danny said Darryl said Morley was an asshole and he meant to teach him some respect. He said they were fighting over you."

"Not really," said Catlyn, embarrassed. "They'd both had too much to drink. It wasn't really about me. You know how guys are."

"Don't I ever," said Sherice and sighed. Catlyn took a close look at her face, but she seemed fine.

On Sunday, Catlyn could already hear the band when she climbed out of the truck at Uncle Teddy's. The rest of the band had started a half hour early to work up a new song. They were rocking—she could hear Grommet whamming on his drums and the electric guitar screaming while she walked through the house. She couldn't tell what the song was until she opened the door to the garage, and the sound hit her full force. Morley was standing in front of the microphone, turned away from her, and he was singing Keith Urban's *Faster Car*, a new song for the band. He was worked up into a state of frenzy, howling into the microphone about his need for speed and his need for something else that was not car-related. The band was on fire, every man bent over his instrument with a ferocity Catlyn had not seen before. Again and again, the band worked toward the final rousing conclusion of the song, only to turn back for another round. Morley vibrated in front of the microphone, growling and yipping. Only when it seemed as though they would either expire or explode, did the band head down the coda and wind things up with some final bangs and cheers. Morley yowled and turned, catching sight of her.

"Well, that was good for me," he said, grinning.

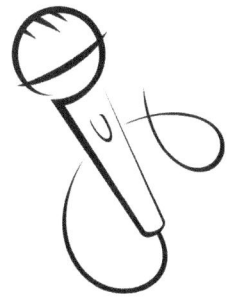

CHAPTER SIX

When Catlyn came into the Cuppa on Tuesday morning, she found Sherice standing in front of the big oven, staring at it and twisting a towel in her hand.

"What's up?" said Catlyn.

"It's broken," Sherice said. "It won't turn on."

"Did Bo come and look at it?" said Catlyn.

"He said it would cost too much to fix it. He said I need a new one," said Sherice.

"How much is that going to be?" asked Catlyn.

"Two thousand bucks," said Sherice.

"Ouch," said Catlyn. They both stared at the oven. Without it, they couldn't make the baked goods that the Cuppa sold along with coffee. And they both knew that was where the Cuppa made its money. No one in Upton was willing to pay three dollars for coffee like they charged in the cities. The Cuppa barely broke even on its 99-cent coffee. But they could eke out a small profit on the cookies, brownies and muffins they served.

"Would Jerry be willing to put in some money?" asked Catlyn.

"I already asked," said Sherice. "He said no."

"Some kind of partner you got there," said Catlyn.

"Tell me about it," sighed Sherice. Jerry was Sherice's cousin, or something like that—Catlyn had never been sure since he almost never showed up and seemed completely uninterested in the coffee shop. He was the original owner and had brought in Sherice a few years ago when he realized that she was willing to work six days a week while he hung out at home or whatever it was he did.

As customers started filing in, Sherice and Catlyn sold the leftover goods from the day before, and when those ran out, Catlyn hustled over to the IGA. She laid out the store-bought muffins, but the regular crowd looked at them with suspicion, especially when Sherice explained that the oven was broken.

"Better get a new one," said one of the guys who worked for the water district. "We need our sugar fix." The other customers in line laughed. Sherice was quiet that morning, and she and Catlyn didn't say much during their cigarette break.

"How are things going with the Pitchforks?" Sherice asked.

"Good, actually," said Catlyn. "Practice went pretty well."

"That Morley guy still making you mad?" teased Sherice.

"Every chance he gets," admitted Catlyn. Sherice pointed out that she didn't sound that peeved about it.

That evening, Catlyn had finished the dishes and was messing around with her notebooks in her room when Sherice called.

"Hey," said Catlyn.

"Don't get mad," said Sherice.

"Now what," said Catlyn, but she smiled.

"I have an idea about how to get the money for the oven," said Sherice.

"How," said Catlyn.

"What if—just think about this for a second before you say anything—what if you come sing one night at the shop, you know, like a benefit, and we can use the money for the oven."

"Sing?" Catlyn couldn't keep the astonishment out of her voice.

"Well, yeah, that's what you do, right?"

"Not like that," Catlyn objected.

"What do you mean? I heard you. You're great."

"I can't just sing. What am I gonna do—sing a cappella? Ah-ah-ah," she yodeled into the phone. "How weird would that be."

"Oh." Sherice paused. "Well, don't you play guitar or something?"

"No, Sherice, I don't just play guitar or something. Anyway, no way."

"Why not?"

"Because no one would come listen to me."

"Now, that's not true," said Sherice vehemently. "You're really good. People would definitely come. Hey, just think about it, okay?"

"No—" started Catlyn.

"We'll talk about it later," said Sherice and hung up.

Catlyn threw herself back on her bed. She wanted to help her friend, but why couldn't she understand that this would never work? Besides, the thought of being in front of a crowd on her own was enough to make her stomach twist in knots.

When she showed up at the Cuppa the next day, Sherice bounced out of the storeroom holding an oversized sheet of paper.

"Look what I made!" She showed Catlyn the paper. It was an advertisement. "Benefit Concert!" it announced. "For the Cuppa's New Oven! One Night Only! Cate Jackson of the Rusty Pitchforks!" Sherice had apparently gone through her photos and pulled out one of Catlyn.

It was a good shot; even Catlyn had to agree; it showed her in slight profile, smiling widely at someone to the side, her blond hair curling on her shoulder.

"Sherice…" Catlyn tailed off. She didn't know what to say.

"Please say yes," said Sherice. "Please please please."

How could Catlyn say no to this full-on onslaught?

"I'll figure something out," she said to her friend.

After rehearsal on Thursday, she approached Morley.

"I need your help," she began, all businesslike.

Morley turned. "Thought you'd never ask," he teased and gave the guys a wink. Catlyn's courage almost failed her.

"I'm serious," she said weakly.

"So am I," he said. "As serious as a heart attack."

She lost her nerve and stepped toward the door.

"Hey, what," Morley said, and his voice softened.

"You remember Sherice?" she said. "From the other night? The one who manages the Cuppa?"

"Sure," Morley said.

"She needs a new oven, you know, for the shop. And she doesn't have the money. And she's trying to get me to sing, to do a benefit," Catlyn said, going faster the more she said. "And I can't because—and I know the 'Forks can't, but I was wondering if…"

"If what," said Morley.

"I mean, I don't know," said Catlyn wildly. "I just thought maybe you could help."

"You want me to accompany you on the guitar?" guessed Morley.

"What? No," said Catlyn, horrified.

"And sing backup for you?" he added and grinned.

"No!" said Catlyn, even more horrified.

"Because I can do that," he said calmly.

"Wait! No, that's not—" said Catlyn.

"Sure, set it up," he said and walked over to get his jacket.

"That's not what I meant," she said flustered.

"It's no problem," he said kindly.

Catlyn was beyond confused. She was irritated, cornered, and frustrated. And was Uncle Teddy hiding a smirk as he put his guitar away? She flounced out of the room. This was getting to be a habit.

The next day, Morley texted her: *When's practice?* She stared at the message in confusion. Did he mean to text Uncle Teddy? He knew when rehearsals were, Sundays and Thursdays without fail. What was going on? Then her phone rang. Her phone said MORLEY on its little screen. Seeing his name gave her a jolt.

"Hello?" she answered.

"Hey, Cat," his deep voice came over the speaker. She had never talked to him on the phone before. His voice sounded nice. *Nestlé Crunch,* she thought. She was considering this when he broke into her thoughts.

"When are we getting together?"

"We getting?" she said, incoherently.

"Practice," he said. "For your gig."

"Oh, ah," she said.

"Did you think we were just going to wing it?"

"Well…"

"I don't think that would be advisable."

"No—"

"Fine. How about tonight? Your uncle's. Six."

"Er—"

"Good."

He hung up. Catlyn thought about her schedule, hoping that she was busy, but in fact she was free that evening. She called home and asked her mother if she could handle the chores.

"Of course, honey, no problem," Marie said. "You got a date?"

"A date? No!" said Catlyn, then more calmly, "I'll tell you later."

"Sure. Since it's not a date," said her mother, and Catlyn could hear the amusement in her voice.

Morley had already prepared the room when Catlyn got to Uncle Teddy's. He'd pulled a couple chairs together and set up a music stand where they could both see it. On it, he had loaded a couple of thick songbooks, some country classics and folk songs. He was carrying a guitar Catlyn had never seen before.

"Just my old beater," he said. "Now, what are you thinking for your set list?"

"I—" He looked at her expectantly.

"We can do them in any order you want," he said helpfully.

"Hm—"

"We should work them up though."

"Er—"

"I had a couple ideas."

"Oh—"

"What about doing an acoustic version of *Joe's Place*? You might have to cheat on some of the notes, but it's easy to sing, and…"

Half an hour later, they had the beginning of a list. Morley had added *Don't Think Twice* and a Joni Mitchell song because he said it was illegal to play a gig in a coffee shop without playing a Joni Mitchell song.

"How about *Gentle on My Mind?*" he suggested. "Solid classic." She agreed. She'd sung that song since she was five.

"I think you should do *American Pie,*" he said.

"Oh, it's too long," she objected.

"We'll shorten it. Come on, it'll go over well." It was a great song, Catlyn knew, a work of genius, really.

"Plus I can play it," Morley added.

"I'm afraid I won't remember the words though," she added. It occurred to her how weak it sounded to say that to someone who had to remember the words to fill three sets of music on a long Saturday night.

"I just fake it when I can't remember," he said. "No one notices."

"Except the girl who listens to *I Feel Lucky* every day on her way to work," said Catlyn.

"Right, except for her," said Morley.

Catlyn shyly suggested *The Lucky One*, one of her favorite Alison Krauss songs.

"Great song," he agreed. He noodled around with it on the guitar and then made a face at her. "Too hard for me to pick though. I can strum, but it won't sound as good as if your uncle were playing."

"That's okay," she said quickly. "Hey, I really appreciate—" He cut her off.

"I think we should take along a music stand. You won't need it, but it might look good."

Catlyn couldn't help but notice how he treated her like a professional, working with her the way he did with Uncle Teddy, making suggestions and listening carefully to her ideas.

"Morley, you know we won't be paid, right?" she said finally.

"I'm shocked."

Of course, Morley had been absolutely right about the crowd's reaction to their dancing on stage. On Saturday night, in the second set, during the guitar solo of *Why Don't We Just Dance,* Morley executed a perfect Elvis-style sliding hip move to slither across the stage and extend a hand to Catlyn. The crowd started yelling and burst into cheers when Catlyn moved out from behind the microphone to join him in front of the band. When he pulled her to him and twirled her, there was a loud wolf whistle from the back and Morley arched a suggestive eyebrow at her. She felt the heat of his body under the lights and the flush from her own skin as they moved around the stage. *In front of God and everybody,* she thought. Suddenly, she didn't care. It was fun to dance with Morley and share the limelight. Her feet moved under her like magic, and she relished Morley's strong hands guiding her, so much so that she was a little disappointed when he deposited her back behind her microphone and slid back to his own to finish up the song. She glanced at the band, and Bo was clearly grinning as he plucked his bass. Even Uncle Teddy looked like he was smiling behind that beard. She looked into the crowd and saw Darryl and Wendi waving to her and giving her thumbs up. It was so unusual to see Darryl laughing she had to look twice. Morley just had a way of bringing good times to people. *To me too,* she thought.

The Cuppa was abuzz in the days leading up to the concert. Sherice had printed up new posters that added *with Morley Graham!* and posted them in the windows. Customers told Catlyn they were looking forward to the show when they ordered their coffee and asked if she could deliver it with a tune.

"Or just hum a little," one kidded her while the others in line chuckled. Catlyn smiled at the jokes, but a feeling of dread filled her every time she thought about the upcoming event.

On Friday night before the benefit concert, Catlyn and Morley got together for another practice at Uncle Teddy's house. Morley made lots of suggestions, and Catlyn wrote down her final selection of songs. They were singing smoothly together by now, between the practices for the Rusty Pitchforks and the sessions they had snuck in for her gig. Catlyn could hear how their voices were becoming more accustomed to each other, and sometimes when their sound came together, she was moved by the sweetness. Morley was mostly business during the sessions, working on details and admonishing her for inconsistent starts or sloppy note transitions. Tonight however, he pronounced her ready.

"I'll pick you up," he said and left without waiting for an answer.

He arrived at Uncle Teddy's early, and they loaded microphones, speakers, monitors, cables and the music rack into his truck without saying much. Once they were driving toward the coffee shop, he turned to her and grinned.

"Let's go get that oven," he said.

A few tables were already filled when they arrived to set up the equipment. Sherice rushed over, beaming when they walked into the kitchen.

"I've already raised a hundred dollars," she said and opened her hand to show them a wad of crumbled bills.

"I feel dirty already," said Morley.

An hour later, they had the equipment set up, the cords taped down, and water bottles at the ready. Sherice had dimmed the lights, but Catlyn could see that nearly every table was full of faces staring in her direction. She was about to pass out from stage fright. She and Morley took their seats, and Sherice came out to introduce them. She was almost as nervous as Catlyn.

"First, thank you so much for coming," she said, and her voice quavered with emotion. "I knew I lived in a really nice town, but to see everyone come out like this…" She sniffed.

"How soon till cookies?" someone called from the back. The crowd laughed.

"Soon as you all get that oven in," Sherice called back. She had recovered herself and turned to introduce Catlyn.

"This is my friend, Cate Jackson. Most of you know her already—I mean, since—well—she works here. I don't know if you know, but she also sings with the Rusty Pitchforks, and she's really good," she ended enthusiastically. There was an awkward pause as the audience waited for her to introduce Morley.

"Enjoy the evening. And thanks again." She departed suddenly by walking back behind the counter. There was another pause.

"I'm Bob Dylan!" Morley shouted and put his hand in the air in greeting. The crowd cracked up and yelled back, "Yeah, Dylan!" They all turned toward Catlyn in anticipation. The only sound was of people shuffling and cups rattling. Catlyn was frozen, staring at the exit door. A buzzing filled her ears.

"Our first number," Morley said *sotto voce* into the microphone, "the sounds of Cuppa." The crowd laughed again, and Morley moved to whisper in Catlyn's ear.

"Are you going to sing or do I have to kiss you in front of all these people?"

Catlyn jerked in surprise and began to fuss with the music rack to cover her shock. It *was* helpful to have something in front of her.

"I thought that would work," he said off-mike with a grin.

They opened with *Joe's Place*, and Morley smoothly filled in when her breath or memory failed her. The homey tune set the mood, and people ordered more coffee and settled in. By the time they finished their third song, Catlyn had recovered sufficiently to be able to look around. Sherice had put out flowers and strung little white lights around the windows. The effect was enchanting, turning the everyday coffee shop into a cozy den full of color and community spirit.

Every table was full, and Catlyn began to pick out individual faces among the blur facing her. She saw her parents, Robert sporting his black cowboy hat, and her mother wearing her hair up in a chignon. She saw Darryl in the back although it looked like he was on his phone. Wendi must be around somewhere. A bunch of the Cuppa regulars were sitting together on the right, kidding each other and guffawing. She was surprised to see Bo there with his wife. He waggled his fingers when she spotted him, and she waggled back, equally reassured and unnerved to see him. Some of the roadhouse girls were there, probably hoping for a few moments' contact with the great Morley. She also noticed some younger kids, probably high school students, too young to get into the roadhouse.

When they came back after the break, Catlyn remembered her manners. "This is Morley Graham," she said. "I appreciate him accompanying me this evening."

"Go, Dylan," called someone in the audience. Morley waved in response.

"How 'bout Dylan sings one," someone shouted from the back. Catlyn was embarrassed that hadn't occurred to her. "I would love that," she burst out, making a few people in the front smile at her. "Would you?"

"Thought you'd never ask," Morley said. He strummed his guitar for a few moments, thinking. "*Maggie's Farm*," someone called.

"*Freebird*," called a wag.

"This one's better," he said. She didn't recognize it until the second line, and then realized it was Brad Paisley's *Letter to Me*, his song to his seventeen-year-old self, telling him that things would get better, that these were *not* the best years of his life. Morley's thoughtfulness for the young people in the audience touched Catlyn, and when the song wound up, she saw tears in a few eyes, more in those of mothers though than seventeen-year-olds. After he got a nice round of applause, Morley pointed to the collection basket and called out, "Oven money goes right up here!" The crowd laughed and some people passed up bills.

"How about we try *The Lucky One*," Morley said in her ear. They had worked it up, and she cherished the song. She had been nervous about how fast it was, but now she felt brave enough to take it on. The crowd was rapt as she sang. Morley's voice chimed in on the chorus to caress hers. *Satin frosting*, she thought. It struck her that the song was well-suited to him. He did seem to embody that carefree approach to life. She noticed that he was picking the song, and his fingers were running fluidly over the strings. He must have learned that since their last practice. *For me*, she thought. *He did that for me.* It sounded great. His face was so close to hers, she could see golden flecks in his eyes that she had never noticed before. He caught her looking at him, and he dropped her the subtlest of winks, causing her to flush despite herself.

He had been right about *American Pie*. As soon as they picked up on the opening notes, the crowd let out a collective sigh of nostalgia. And when Catlyn and Morley slowed it down for the final chorus, the crowd softly joined in. Their voices raised together, with his guitar thrumming gently, the song seemed to transport them, the crowd, the coffee shop, even the oven, into a storybook moment. Catlyn felt a burst of gratitude, for her town, for the Cuppa, for Sherice, and—she had to admit—for Morley. Suddenly, singing together with him at this show seemed like the best thing she'd ever done in her life, and her heart filled.

When the show was over, as she and Morley were breaking down equipment, Catlyn looked up to see Darryl and Wendi standing over them. She startled but heard Morley say casually, "Hey."

"Hey," said Darryl. "I just wanted to say, about the other night—"

"Yeah," said Morley, "I can be an asshole sometimes."

"Yeah, I'd had a few," said Darryl.

"Can you unplug that cable for me," said Morley. And then Darryl was helping Morley take down the equipment and pack it into his truck. Catlyn and Wendi looked at each other and shook their heads.

When Sherice counted out the money, they had raised a whopping $1,725; one person had put in a one-hundred-dollar bill, and Catlyn suspected her dad of that generous act. With what Sherice had been putting aside over the past couple weeks, she said she could get the new oven. She couldn't stop hugging Catlyn and Morley. Morley looked pleased as punch.

"Free baked goods for life?" he asked.

Later, in Catlyn's room at Uncle Teddy's, Morley asked, "By the way, did Sherice get a performance license for the coffee shop?"

"What does that mean?" Catlyn asked.

"It allows performers to play cover songs at the venue," he said. "It's to make sure that songwriters get paid for their songs."

She stared at him. "I have no idea," she said. "Is it expensive?"

"Yes," he said.

"Well, I don't know. Is it important?"

"Only if you think it's important that songwriters get paid for their songs."

"I do think that's important."

"Guess you're in trouble now," he said and grinned at her. "It's not just illegal to perform someone's song without getting a license; it's theft." He opened his eyes wide and stared at her. Catlyn was appalled. Although people in her neck of the woods had a healthy skepticism of the law, Catlyn and her parents were generally law-abiding folk.

"I didn't know," she sputtered. "I feel terrible."

"It *is* terrible," Morley said. "Right now, I can see Joni Mitchell crying in her big house because Cate Jackson performed her song, and she didn't get the twenty-five cents that she was supposed to."

Catlyn stared at him. Was he pulling her leg?

"Twenty-five cents?" She stared at him confused. He nodded soberly and looked very sad. Suddenly, she whacked him on the arm. "I thought you were serious!" she protested.

"Bob Dylan," he said and shook his head. "Don McLean. All victims," he mourned.

Catlyn started laughing, and he grabbed her by the wrist and pulled her down on the bed. She shrieked in mock surprise, and he covered her mouth with his hand.

"Cat burglar," he whispered. "I caught you." They lay quietly for a moment.

"Can I ask you something?" she said.

"Maybe," he said.

"Would you like to come out to the farm to have dinner with my parents?"

"I thought you'd never ask."

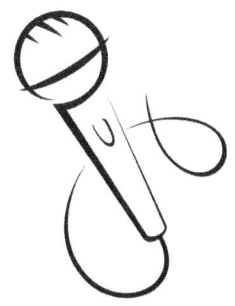

CHAPTER SEVEN

On Sunday, Uncle Teddy announced that the Pitchforks had been invited to play on July Fourth at the county fairgrounds. The event was likely to draw a big crowd, and the band quickly signed on even though it was a work night. Since they had the set before the fireworks began, a prime time, they would be finished before nine o'clock. It would be more of a sit-down event with chairs set up in front of an outside stage, and the band discussed some different song choices for the new format. Morley, of course, had an opinion.

"I think we need some duets," he said. "In fact," he continued, "I think we should get her out front where people can see her." And to make his point, he dragged Catlyn's microphone up next to his and set it down with a thump.

"There," he said. Catlyn started to object.

"That's a good idea," said Uncle Teddy, "It'll be something new in case the roadhouse folks come to see us—which they will." And that was that. The band started throwing out ideas for duets.

"I like that new song *Better Find a Church*," said Bo.

"Oo, me too," said Catlyn.

"I'd like to see you two sing *Jackson*," said Uncle Teddy, naming Johnny Cash's and June Carter's famous tune.

"How about *It's Different for Girls*?" Woody said suddenly. They all turned and stared at him. Then Catlyn remembered that he had two grown daughters.

"That is an excellent suggestion," said Morley. "In fact, those are all great—in my opinion." He then added quickly. "What do you think, Cat?" Catlyn looked around at the band, touched.

"I think they are fabulous," she said. "And I'll see you in Jackson," she said to Morley, "you big-talkin' man." The band snickered. Morley said they they should come up with a new solo for Catlyn to sing in the first set. *I Feel Lucky* was starting to sound old.

"How about *I Can't Even Get the Blues*?" suggested Uncle Teddy.

"Oh, yes," said Catlyn. She used to sing the old Reba McEntire song with Uncle Teddy when they drove in the truck, and she still enjoyed the sarcastic lyrics. Even Grommet was laughing at her delivery after the first run through. Catlyn was feeling more and more like part of the band now. They even gave her a tambourine to play on *Pink Houses*. She waved it around vaguely during practice.

"Don't do that," said Morley, stopping the song. "Show her how to really play that thing," he told Grommet who climbed out from behind his drum set to show her how to strike and shake the tambourine with precision. After a little work, he pronounced her "pretty much as good as Kenny Aronoff."

"Maybe we should teach her to play the harmonica," Bo mused.

"Hey, hands off my singer," Morley groused.

On the day Morley was supposed to come for dinner, he texted Catlyn while she was at the Cuppa: *Pick u up where when*

"Will miracles never cease," Catlyn told Sherice. "I believe it's the first time he hasn't given me a direct order." Sherice cackled.

"You might tame him after all."

Morley picked Catlyn up at Uncle Teddy's after she had gathered her things for the weekend. She hopped into his truck and looked around. The truck was well-used but orderly, and it had a good stereo system and a stack of CDs sitting on the console. A Merle Haggard song was playing. One of the things she liked about Morley was that he wasn't biased about contemporary country music versus the old stuff. If someone brought in a new song, he would give it a chance, no matter what era it came from. That worked well at The Corral since it drew a crowd of all ages and the Pitchforks needed to appeal to the whole range. She felt the same way: a good song was a good song, no matter what year it was written.

She sat back, listening to Merle lament the troubles that face the everyday man, and watched Morley out of the corner of her eye. He drove smoothly, his hands relaxed on the wheel. She studied those hands, the narrow fingers with neat nails, and the golden hairs that decorated his knuckles and arms. His hands were sure and fluid as they moved the wheel and controls, and she couldn't help but imagine what else those hands could do. The afternoon sun shining in the cab and the warmth of her daydreams put her in a reverie which she snapped out of when Morley spoke.

"Penny for your thoughts?" he asked and slid his eyes over to meet hers. She started and looked out the window. Had he guessed what she had been daydreaming about, while watching him drive?

"Oh nothing," she stuttered.

"Fine—a dime then," he said.

"Well," she said, thinking to herself that it *was* possible to have two thoughts at the same time. "I was thinking about how the first time I heard Joe Nichols I couldn't believe how much he sounded like Merle Haggard."

"Uh-huh," he said and smiled knowingly. Then, "And?"

"And, well, but—I guess there's no one like Merle Haggard."

"How so?" said Morley.

"He's got a twang sometimes to his voice—a kind of hardness, but sometimes he sounds really melodic too."

"He wasn't so worried about always sounding pretty the way we do today. It's hard to switch back and forth the way he does."

"You can do it," said Catlyn.

"I try," said Morley.

"How did you learn to do all the different things with your voice?" said Catlyn.

"A lot of time alone," he said. "I've spent a lot of time alone, Cat."

She thought about his room in the basement, the guitar and the music sheets everywhere. She wondered if it would pay off for him someday.

When they got out of the truck at the farm, Catlyn pointed out the land that belonged to her parents.

"Whoa! Look at all those plants," Morley said.

"Those are soybeans," she said. It was almost July, and the plants were doing well so far. The hard part would come later; it was always a worry about whether it would rain in late summer or if the drought of the past few years would continue.

"Soy beans," Morley said, looking puzzled. She had to laugh. He made it sound like a new food.

He turned to consider the one-story ranch house with its neat yard and two colorful flower gardens out front and the big barn up the way.

"So, this is home," he said, and his tone was neutral. Catlyn tried to see the homestead through his eyes, but who knew what a Californian would think of this little place. It was all her family had even though it didn't look like much. Just then, however, the front door opened, and

Marie popped out, wearing an apron and a big smile, welcoming them inside.

After introductions were made, she suggested Robert take Morley out to look at the new tractor while Marie and Catlyn got supper on. Morley blinked but recovered quickly.

"I'd like to see a tractor up close," he said. "As long as it doesn't harvest me or whatever it does."

Good, thought Catlyn, *he should spend some time with an Upton man. Might teach him something.*

Morley paused by the hat rack on the way out the side door and picked up Rob's black cowboy hat.

"Is this your work hat?" he asked.

"Ah… no," chuckled Robert.

"What do you wear when you work?" persisted Morley.

"A baseball cap, son. Farmers wear baseball caps when they work."

"What's that hat for then?"

"That hat is for dancing."

Eavesdropping, Marie and Catlyn turned to each other and silently shook with mirth.

After the screen door had slammed behind the guys, Marie spoke. "Oh, *honey*," she said to her daughter, widening her eyes. "Oh, *my*, honey, is he ever good-looking."

"I know," said Catlyn. "It's kind of… distracting."

"Distracting," said her mother pensively. "Cate, there will come a time when it won't be distracting at all." And she arched her eyebrows suggestively and smiled.

"Mom!" Catlyn tried to look shocked, but she knew her mother had a sexy side. Besides any red-blooded heterosexual woman would react that way to Morley.

Dinner went well. Morley ate enough for two teenagers which delighted Marie, and she bustled around him, making sure he had plenty of lasagna and salad. He managed to inhale four pieces of garlic bread, compliment Marie's cooking, ask Rob about soybeans, joke about rush hour in Upton, and squeeze in some sidelong glances at Catlyn. After apple pie, he conceded defeat and declared Marie the winner. She giggled like a girl. Even Robert seemed amused by this vivacious charmer from California. It was nearly dark by the time dinner was over, and Marie shooed them out of the kitchen to go sit on the porch.

"Your mom's a good cook," Morley declared. He collapsed on the swing and stuck his feet out. Catlyn settled beside him. It occurred to her that he might not have had much chance for a home-cooked meal since moving to Upton.

"Thanks for coming," she said shyly. "My parents really enjoyed meeting you."

"You're very lucky," he said, suddenly fierce. "I hope you—" She heard his breath catch in his throat.

"Morley?" she said. "Is everything okay?" She peered into his face and almost thought she saw a glisten in one eye.

"Let's go for a walk," he said roughly and pulled her to her feet. It was too dark to head to the barn, so they set off down the driveway where the gravel shone a ghostly white. *Our path is lit; We can walk a bit*, she thought.

They didn't say anything for a while. Catlyn wanted to talk but decided to wait him out. The fireflies were out, and she loved how they floated around in the dark, reappearing like little intrepid lanterns.

"This is nice," he said and took her hand. Catlyn noticed again how warm his hand was. When Morley held your hand, the feeling went all the way up your arm.

"I'm glad," she said and squeezed his hand.

"It's just—your family—you're really lucky," he said again and cleared his throat.

"I know," she said quietly. *Wait*, she told herself, *wait*.

"My mother's kind of got her own thing going on," he said finally. "And I don't have much to do with my dad."

"Is he some kind of Hollywood mogul?" she asked.

"Hardly," he snorted. "Just your ordinary jerk. Anyway, they're divorced now."

Catlyn held herself back from jumping down his throat with more questions. It was the first time he'd opened up about his life, if you could call that opening up, and she held her breath to see if more was coming. Apparently not, because he whistled a little and swung her hand.

"Morley," she said finally. "You have my family now."

He stopped and looked at her. "That's very generous of you," he said and smiled. "Does your dad know I have no idea how to drive a tractor?"

"I'll teach you," she said and smiled back. Lifting her chin in the moonlight, he looked in her eyes and let his gaze run over her face.

"I'd like to teach you a few things," he said and casually stroked her arms, raising goosebumps on her skin. Catlyn was aware of how close he was standing to her, but she didn't step back. He moved even closer and raised his hands to her face, then slid them behind her neck. He leaned in to kiss her, and Catlyn tasted his lips and felt the pressure and warmth of his chest against hers in the chilly night air. A rush of heat ran through her body, and she trembled. Morley pulled his lips away, but only slightly, and rested his forehead against hers. He moved closer still and pressed against her. Catlyn sensed the strength in his arms and the power of that compact body. She could feel his legs and the hardness between them, and it sent an electric surge of sexual desire through her. She almost staggered, but Morley moved his arms around her and pulled her close. She leaned in for a kiss and felt for his lips, his mouth, his tongue. He obliged by moving his lips apart, and she felt the moist heat inside. He rocked her body against his, and she almost moaned as desire spread.

"Mmmm," he said appreciatively and leaned back for a breath of air. "M-M-M," he added and moved a hand down to her waist and then lower. But he loosened his grip, and Catlyn detected that the moment was coming to an end. Suddenly conscious of the time, the dark, and the warmth between her legs, she stepped back, but not before Morley slipped in a squeeze, one that she would remember. She took a shaky breath and said, "I guess we should get back."

They walked back to his truck, and Morley pulled her in for a last kiss. Catlyn felt her breath coming fast as he held his body hard against her.

"There are lots more things to learn," he whispered.

He turned to put her back against the truck and slipped a hand inside her jacket while his lips met hers again. Catlyn felt a little light-headed, and he steadied her elbow as he stepped back. She didn't think her parents would be looking out the windows, but she was aware of the porch light lighting up the romantic tableau, as though they were actors on a stage. *The kiss*, she thought, and then her mind went blank. Morley opened the door to his truck and slid in. He put the window down and looked out at her with a smile playing around the edge of his lips.

"I'm glad the cat knows how to play," he said huskily and tapped the side of the truck before he started the engine.

After she was in her room, Catlyn had just taken out her earphones when she heard her mother and father in their room next to hers.

"So, what did you think?" Marie asked.

"I thought he was okay. Could use a haircut. What's more important is what you thought," said Catlyn's father.

"I liked him," said Marie. "I mean he does have that God's gift to women thing going on, but—"

"It's not his fault that he looks like that."

"True… The thing is—I wonder how old he is."

"He's 24. I asked him."

"You asked him? Are you even allowed to ask people how old they are now?"

"I wanted to know. I asked. He told me."

Catlyn stifled a laugh in her pillow. How much did her dad sound like Morley right now? But 24? She squeezed her eyes shut. She figured he was older than she was, but she didn't think—well, she was hoping—that he wasn't so much older. He was a man really. Thinking of his body against hers gave her a sharp flash of pleasure.

"Six years," said her mother. "Oh, Robert, that's a lot."

"It seems like a lot now, but it won't in thirty years."

"Planning ahead, aren't you?"

"You gotta start somewhere. And Cate has a good head on her shoulders. She's mature for her age."

"Compared to him though, she's awfully young. He's been around. We don't really know much about him. Did you notice he dodged the question about his family? I just worry—"

"Bottom line, I like him. He's inquisitive, seems honest, and he can't seem to breath right when she's in the same room."

"Yes, he's smitten. So cute. I liked him too."

"Okay, so how 'bout we let the young people figure their own love lives out, and we spend a little time on our own."

Catlyn heard her mother laugh low and the bed creak and decided it was a good time to stick her headphones back in. She thought about what her parents had said. Of course her dad would think she was capable of anything, but she knew her mom could see right inside her to that little girl who still lived there. Well, maybe it was time for that little girl to grow up. And she had an idea of who could help her with that.

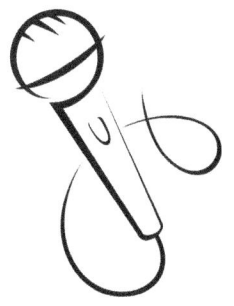# CHAPTER EIGHT

In preparation for the July Fourth show, Catlyn and Morley decided to try out some of their new material in the next performance at the roadhouse. The crowd was captivated by their humorous exchange on *Jackson*. When they traded off the Johnny Cash and June Carter parts, the crowd seemed to draw closer, pulled in by the rapport between them. Although Catlyn relished singing in front of the crowd with Morley, she still felt like an impostor at the microphone. Morley was such a pro. When she watched him work the crowd and sing his heart out, there was a small voice inside her that said *You are not like him—you are not fearless like that.*

Morley had no such qualms. He decided that Catlyn needed to learn how to sing harmony, so he took it upon himself to give her some lessons. She could fake her way through most parts, but a few of the songs they were doing now required real harmony singing. Morley explained how to count two notes up from the melody to find the harmony. He showed her how to cover her ear closest to him so she could hear herself.

"The most important thing to be able to hear it in your head," he said. "Even when you're not singing, you should practice that."

"Practice in my head?" said Catlyn.

"You can't sing it if you can't hear it," Morley said. "Besides it's fun. It passes the time."

The thought of Morley passing the time by singing in his head amused Catlyn. That said, she did love singing harmony with him, and the wonderful mix of their voices sometimes brought tears to her eyes.

"It's lovely," she said, after one song. "I don't know why, but it's beautiful."

"Yeah, baby," said Morley. "I could tell you a bunch of stuff about triads and dissonance, but all that matters is how does it make you feel," Morley said. He snapped his fingers and did a twirl. "*Does the tune make you croon?*" he sang.

July Fourth dawned bright and hot. Marie had agreed to do the evening chores so Catlyn could go to the fairgrounds early. Catlyn hurried through the morning feeding so she had time to get ready. She'd thought about wearing the yellow dress just to see what Morley would say, but Sherice had helped her pick out a black slinky dress with roses on it. Catlyn liked the colors, but Sherice said it was a good choice because she looked smokin' hot in it. Catlyn smiled at the recollection while she got ready. She was a little nervous because she and Morley had so many new songs, but she couldn't wait to be up on the stage again with the band.

The show was fun although different. Since it was still daylight, she could see the crowd, and the lights weren't as hot. It was like performing at a picnic. She enjoyed seeing the crowd and watching them tap their feet and bob their heads. Her parents were there too, giving her a wave or thumbs up when she looked their way.

During *New Chick in the Henhouse*, when Uncle Teddy was wailing away on the guitar, she couldn't resist playing a little air guitar. As though he had read her mind, Morley joined in at the same instant and the two of jammed until Uncle Teddy noticed what was happening and came up to join them in a line. The crowd loved the spectacle and whistled in appreciation.

When the solo part of *Why Don't We Just Dance* came along, Morley hip-slid over behind the drum set before he headed her way, putting Robert's black hat on his head. The crowd yelled its approval, and Catlyn looked at him wonderingly. She hadn't noticed that Robert wasn't wearing his hat. There was no time to look at him as she was being twirled around the stage but once back behind her microphone she looked out at her father. He gave her a hats-off gesture, with no hat, and grinned.

The crowd laughed and crowed during *Jackson*, and Catlyn saw her mother nod and whisper to her dad during *It's Different for Girls*. Morley was once again hailed as the hero. As the band's last number wound down, he took Catlyn by the hand and twirled her a time or two around the stage. The crowd was less boisterous (and drunk) than the roadhouse gang but more persistent. Even after the band had headed offstage, the audience continued to clap and whistle. There were no house lights to signal that the band was definitely not coming back again, and the band was nonplussed. They'd never been invited out for an encore before. If they played a minute past midnight at the roadhouse, the local do-gooders might try to get somebody arrested.

"Let's just take the two of you and me back out there," said Uncle Teddy, "and we'll play something." Bo, Woody, and Grommet looked relieved. The gig had been fun, but they were tired and ready to head out for the drive back to Upton. It was left to the last three standing to bring it home. The crowd cheered when the three of them reappeared. Morley sprang to the microphone, looking as fresh as he had at the beginning of the evening except for the telltale signs of perspiration.

"You have been an exceptional crowd," he told the audience sincerely. They gave themselves a round of applause.

"We have just one last number for you," he said, "and I hope it's as meaningful to you as it is to me." To Catlyn's surprise, Uncle Teddy moved into the opening chords of *You Are So Beautiful*. She turned to look at Morley who pretended to ignore her. Into the second verse, he took her hand, and the crowd murmured. Catlyn joined in on the chorus, but she mostly listened to Morley's exquisite timing. They closed up the tune, and Morley kissed her as the lights went out. Someone in the crowd wolf-whistled. Catlyn thought it might have sounded like her dad.

After the equipment was broken down, Morley and Catlyn wanted to watch the fireworks, and they told Uncle Teddy they would ride back with Sherice and Danny who were around somewhere, according to their phones. Morley wanted to see the midway of the fair, and he and Catlyn strolled through the booths while their attendants tried to entice Morley to try his luck at shooting hoops or ducks.

"Win your girlie a stuffed bear," called out one.

"I just want to win the girlie," Morley said in her ear, and she giggled. A few people who had seen them singing turned and watched as they went past. Morley was still wearing Robert's hat and cut quite a figure.

"What are those things?" said Morley, pointing to a shaved-ice treat some people were carrying around.

"Those are snow cones," said Catlyn. "Let's get one." After he had taken several bites, Morley declared it "really cold Koolaid in a weird cup." He snuck in a few kisses between bites and claimed that made it taste better.

"Let's go find us some more fireworks," he said and grinned at her. They met up with Sherice and Danny and found a spot on the grass. Sherice had brought a blanket, and the four of them leaned back on their elbows to watch the show. Morley edged his legs close to Catlyn's and put an arm around her back. He bent to kiss her as the first shower of lights opened up above them, and she tasted liquor on his breath. She was surprised to see that he and Danny each had a bottle. The fireworks were amazing for a small county show. As she watched the array of reds, greens, blues, and whites light up the sky above her, she felt a burst of euphoria. Maybe she was the lucky one—how had she ended up in this wonderland of lights with a beautiful boy? When the finale came, Danny and Morley lifted their bottles to the sky, and she and Sherice turned to each other and rolled their eyes.

After they were on their way back to Upton with Sherice behind the wheel, she turned to Morley and Catlyn holding hands in the back seat.

"Where to, lovers?" she said.

"My place," said Morley. He started to give her directions, but she said, "I know where you live." In a small town, word gets around.

"Why? You been there?" asked Danny suddenly and belligerently. He had turned sullen on the drive home, and a cold lump settled in Catlyn's stomach. Sherice turned to him, but it was Morley who spoke first.

"No, she hasn't been there, and I'll thank you to keep that in mind in case—in case, you get any designs on *my* girlfriend," he said primly and then suddenly collapsed in a fit of giggles.

Danny stared at him and then said slowly, "Okay, well, I'll thank you to—to keep in mind which girlfriend is mine!" He started laughing too. His dark moment seemed to have passed.

"Okay," said Morley, "and I'll thank you, Sherice—for a ride home."

"I'll thank you—" Danny began, but he couldn't finish because he was wheezing with laughter. Sherice caught Catlyn's eye in the rearview mirror and shook her head, but she was smiling.

When they got to Mrs. Scales' house, Morley leaned over to Catlyn.

"Why don't you come in," he said, and it wasn't a question. She hesitated, but he opened the door and pulled on her hand.

"Ah, why not," he said and grinned at her. "You don't have to regret it until morning."

"You don't have to—" said Danny and began laughing again.

She went to open Mrs. Scales' door, but Morley beat her to it.

"After you," he said, still smiling at her.

She slid past him and headed down the stairs, hoping Mrs. Scales wouldn't hear. Morley clicked on the switch which illuminated the single lightbulb over the hot plate and refrigerator. The place looked exactly the same as she had seen it last time except that Morley wasn't wearing a jacket and it wasn't their opening night. She paused in the middle of the mostly bare room, and Morley came up behind her and put his hands on her shoulders. She turned and looked in his face. He had taken Robert's hat off and put it by the door.

"How I have waited for this," he said, and she was almost frightened by the emotion on his face. She would have stepped back if he hadn't put his arms around her. He began kissing her passionately. She gasped at his fervor, and his hot breath warmed her cheek. He stroked her hair and managed to get his shirt off while he continued to kiss her. His chest was covered with soft golden hair, and she ran her hands over his arms and shoulders, feeling her breath grow shallow as desire filled her. He moved a hand behind her back while he unbuttoned the front of her dress.

"Got to get you out of all this," he murmured, and Catlyn realized that he had unhooked her bra. Everything came tumbling forth—her dress, her bra, and her breasts, and Morley took full advantage, caressing and stroking. He pressed her hips against him, and again Catlyn felt his arousal. She suddenly pictured them in her mind's eye, half-naked under the single lightbulb, and the image excited her with its carnality. *Stella!* she thought and at the same moment, *Country songs don't really talk about this.* Morley led her toward the bed, and she let herself go. He sat her on the edge of the bed, eased off her shoes, kicked off his own and slid on top of her.

"Not very romantic lighting," he said, "but you look hot as hell." He slid her out of her dress and unsnapped his jeans. She could taste the liquor on his breath, but his kisses were warm and searching and sweet, and she wanted to put her arms around him and never let go. Events seemed to move of their own accord, and a minute later, they were both naked under the cover. He crooked an arm around her head and moved over her, and she felt him between her legs. Her skin felt hot, and he was talking in her ear, encouraging her, raising her heartbeat. He kissed her again, and keeping his face close to hers, he reached over to the table next to the bed and pulled open a drawer. The next thing she knew he was extracting a condom from its wrapper with surprising efficiency. He laid on his side to roll the condom over his penis while she looked on in astonishment.

"I am not the guy who goes around getting people pregnant," he mumbled. Then he added, "And you do look incredibly fertile." Suddenly, Catlyn laughed. Somehow the whole thing seemed so *Morley*—the swinging lightbulb, the nakedness, the condom, her alleged fertility. Morley looked alarmed at her laughter.

"Is this a good thing?" he asked her, and rubbed against her leg in case it was.

"It is," she said. "Oh, baby, you have no idea," and put her arms around him and raised her legs to embrace him. He responded and bent his head down to kiss her.

"Thank god," he said. "You had me worried. Now, what is it that little girls are made of?

Catlyn arched her back. "Gunpowder and lead," she whispered.

"Damn straight," he murmured and moved in again.

What followed was both sweeter and sweatier than Catlyn had imagined. Morley seemed determined to get the most out of the moment, and he tasted of her again and again. Catlyn was overcome by his passion and enthusiasm and enjoyed every minute. When he finally came, he collapsed on her, and she held him in her arms as carefully as a rare flower.

"That was the best *ever*," he murmured and fell asleep.

Catlyn would have anticipated that Morley would be a light sleeper, that someone with that much quickness and motion would maintain those kinetics during the night. But Morley slept like a man felled. Collapsed on his back with an arm thrown over his head, he breathed deeply and did not stir until the morning light. Catlyn had risen to turn off the lightbulb and crawled back into bed to curl next to him, but he lay snug and solid as she cuddled next to him. *A slumbering bear,* she thought, *an evening so fair*. Then she fell asleep too.

In the morning, she woke before Morley. Her eye fell on Robert's hat still sitting by the door, and she thought of the previous evening and what had changed. She turned to gaze at Morley. She studied his face, his eyebrows and nose. His mouth was slightly open, and she sketched the perfect Cupid's bow of his upper lip with her finger. He murmured something, and she bent her head low over him.

"What?" she whispered.

"Get your paws off me, pussy cat," he said. She looked at him astonished. Then he burst into laughter. "You have no idea how long I've been waiting to say that," he said and spanked her on the butt. She swatted him.

For the next hour, they laid around and talked about the concert and the amazing fireworks. Then talk turned to sex—sex with other people, that is.

"Have you had a lot of girlfriends?" she asked.

"Are you asking my number, Kit Kat?"

"No," she said, embarrassed. "I just—"

"I had a girlfriend in California," he said. "I followed her to Austin. Which was stupid."

"What happened?"

"The usual," he said, with a note of bitterness. "How about you? Did you and Darryl do the dirty deed?" He reached down and stroked her thigh.

"Don't call it that," she said. In fact, she and Darryl *had* gone "all the way," a strange expression when you thought about it. Sure, it wasn't anything like what she'd just experienced with the great Morley, but she felt protective of their eager, awkward fumblings. They had just been kids after all.

"Besides, how did you know—"

"A man doesn't act like that for no reason," he said. "Anyway, I promise *Darryl* that I won't call you 'eye candy' anymore. I'll call you 'sexy mama,' and—" He rolled over on top of her and kissed her mouth, tugging on her lip.

"'a total fox,' and—"

He moved down and slowly sucked on a nipple. Catlyn sharply drew in her breath, and he smiled.

"'a gorgeous piece of ass,' and—" She felt him hard between her legs.

"'fuckable as hell,' and—" She didn't wait to hear anymore.

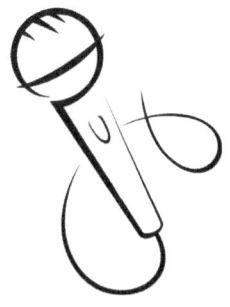 **CHAPTER NINE**

Catlyn needed to get out to the farm to take care of the animals in the morning, and Morley gave her a ride out of town. He suggested that they get together that evening and offered to come pick her up, but she declined. It was one thing to stay with him on a night she would already be in town; it was another to waltz off from the farm to spend the night with a boy. She wasn't sure what her parents would think about that. Morley kissed her deeply in the truck and put a warm hand on her knee before she got out.

"When can I see you again?" he asked.

"I'll see you tomorrow at practice," she said lightly.

"Can you come to my house after?" he asked.

"I can," she said.

"Good," he said. "I think you need to learn a little more about harmonics."

Thursday's practice started with chatter about the July Fourth show, undoubtedly a success. The band was discussing song selection for the next roadhouse gig and debating which of the new material to include. Some of the duets were too slow for the dance-happy roadhouse gang, so those were mothballed for now. Morley suggested that they bring in a new solo for Catlyn that people could slow-dance to.

"You should sing *Blue Ain't Your Color*," Morley said.

"*You* should sing that song," retorted Catlyn. "You would sound great. Besides it's a guy's song."

"It doesn't work for me because you have blue eyes. Besides, that's ridiculous to say it's a guy's song. If it's a good song, sing it."

"Then how come you never sing a girl's song?" she shot back. Morley paused.

"Bring me a good one, and I will," he said.

"You're on!" The band exchanged glances.

"Five bucks she'll make him sing one," Bo murmured to Grommet.

Morley stopped Catlyn on his porch when they got to his house after practice.

"Wait for me here for a second, will you?" He disappeared inside. Catlyn hoped that he would hurry. She didn't want to run into Mrs. Scales while she was loitering on her doorstep, like a lovesick stalker. Morley called up a few minutes later that she could come down. Catlyn stepped off the bottom step and wasn't sure what had happened. The ambiance in the basement was completely different. The single lightbulb was off—that she could see right away. Morley had lit some candles, and music was playing. She hesitated because the room appeared empty.

"Ma'am," said Morley and stepped out from the shadows, wearing his jacket and—hard to believe—a collared shirt. He also had purchased a cowboy hat of his own, a pretty tan-colored number with a golden braid. He held a hand out to her, and Catlyn stepped forward. He moved swiftly to put her in his arms and smiled sexily down at her like some sort of western rake. She yelped and blushed.

"What's that music?" she asked. It wasn't familiar but nice, rhythmic and upbeat.

"That," Morley said, "is salsa—real dance music." He whipped her around and bent her back on her heels. She gasped as it seemed she would fall, but he held her tight. She felt the strength of his chest muscles through his shirt.

"Oh, my," she said, and her throat was dry.

When he let her up, she could see the scene he had laid out. Not only were there candles, the bed was made, and a champagne bottle was sitting on the bedside table, along with two flutes. She had no idea where he could have gotten any of this stuff.

"Champagne, dahling?" he offered with such savoir-faire, that Catlyn giggled. "You don't have to drink," he said suddenly seriously. "I have Sprite too."

"I would love a glass of champagne," she said and drank deeply when he brought her the drink.

"I might have been a bit hasty the other night… So may I have this dance?" he said and extended a hand.

The dancing was fabulous, but within five minutes, Morley was pressed against her.

"Can we dance later?" he asked plaintively, nuzzling her neck.

Catlyn allowed herself once again to be led toward the bed, and Morley slid his hand up around her neck.

"You are the sexiest woman alive," he said and kissed her at length. Catlyn smiled at him. There was no place else she would rather be, and she didn't mind that he knew it. He smiled back and kissed her again, using one hand to unbutton her blouse and the other to hike up her skirt. She moved her hands over his shoulders and began to unbutton his shirt.

"This is very sexy," she whispered to him as she stroked his chest hair under his shirt. It was as though an electric shock went through him then, and he inhaled deeply. With a moan, he pushed her onto the bed and hiked her legs up. Catlyn stretched her arms over her head and slithered out of her blouse. He caressed her breasts and put an arm behind her to unhook her bra. She paused to remove her skirt, and he took a moment to slip out of his jeans. Immediately, Catlyn was aware of how stimulated she was and how she was beyond ready for what she hoped would come. He moved on top of her, and again she felt how hard he was. He paused and gazed at her in the candlelight.

"I know I talk a lot," he said, "but you are beautiful."

"So are you," she said and meant it.

This time she was prepared when he leaned over to reach into his bedside table and pulled out the condom packet. When he flipped the empty packet onto the floor, she chuckled. He sat back and paused, giving her a peek at what was underway.

"Do you want to do the honors?" he asked, watching her closely.

"I do," she said, "but I might need some guidance."

"Honey, I'll take care of the guidance," he said and showed her what she could do. A few moments later, she was caught up in his rhythm and had forgotten any inhibition that might have come before. She arched her back and moaned as he moved inside her. His arms encircled her and his hands caressed her as he kissed and encouraged her. She felt a flame light inside her, small at first and then turning into a real fire. She felt a need for him, and what he could bring her, filling her gradually and more urgently, until she covered her face with her hands.

"Come on, Cat," urged Morley. "Come on." He reached into her again and again while she climbed that wave, each time, a little higher. Sensing her arousal, he stroked between her legs and nuzzled her breasts. No longer bashful, Catlyn offered herself to him and sought relief from the point she had been brought to.

"Now," said Morley and thrust into her. Catlyn gasped and, without knowing why or exactly when, she flew over the edge, and was riding down a roller coaster of thrills, each more exquisite than the last, while she clung to Morley for mooring, until she collapsed, spent, under his weight. He murmured as his legs encircled her, and he moved toward his own resolution. When he came this time, Catlyn could feel the clench and release and rose to meet his moment. She drew a shaky breath and moved her hand to push back her hair. Morley rested his head on her shoulder for a moment.

"Goddam," he said and blew out a breath. She smiled and suddenly giggled and then laughed. He grinned as he looked down at her. She rested her head against his and then kissed him as though it were their first kiss and their last.

"Goddam," he said again and then collapsed on his back next to her. A few minutes later, they were sleeping the sleep of lovers, spells of deep slumber broken by moments of stirring, when they became foggily aware of each other and murmured, when they touched in the dark and, before they fell unconscious again, were briefly thankful.

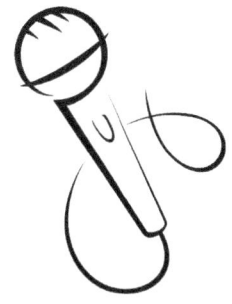

CHAPTER TEN

Catlyn spent more time that week looking for a song for Morley than she cared to admit. But by Saturday, she hadn't come up with anything that she thought was a sure thing. Uncle Teddy happened to come to dinner that evening since it was an off-week at the roadhouse.

"So, Cate, have you found a song for Morley?" he asked. He seemed amused by the challenge that was playing out between the two.

"I haven't," she admitted. "It's harder than I thought it would be."

"I'm not surprised," said Uncle Teddy. "It's not easy to pick a song for someone. What kind of song are you thinking of?"

"I wanna find something that would show him…"

"Show him what?" questioned Uncle Teddy.

"That girls can sing… big songs."

"What do you mean?"

"That girls can sing—songs that are important."

"Ah-ha, now you're onto something. What do you think would be important to Morley?"

She thought about that for a long time. "Family," she said finally.

"Bingo," said Uncle Teddy. "Now you'll figure it out."

He was right. Once Catlyn was on that path, she found *This Boy's Kin,* a song that she thought was a winner. The thing was though, she no longer wanted to shove it down Morley's throat. She just hoped he would actually like it.

When she walked into the garage on Sunday, Morley was already there.

"So, big shot," he said immediately. "What have you got for me?" The rest of the band looked on with interest as she passed out the sheet music.

"What the hell…" Morley muttered. Catlyn glared at him.

"Just try it."

Uncle Teddy ran through the melody, and Bo tried a few chord progressions. Morley sang a few lines.

"Oo," he said in falsetto. "I feel like an asshole."

Bo snickered. "Ooo," he mimicked.

Morley gave him the finger.

"Hey!" said Catlyn. She stared at him. "Sing it!" she ordered.

"Fine, fine," he said. Then, "You know what?" and he turned to the microphone with determination. Catlyn could tell that he had started the song in defiance, to show her something. She held her breath. It wasn't until the second verse that she could see it hit him. His voice faltered, and she thought he was going to stop the song. She joined him at the microphone and softly began singing in unison with him. When the song was finished, there was a long silence. He turned to her and looked her in the eye.

"You win," he said.

"Dammit," said Grommet, who had just lost five bucks.

The next weekend at the roadhouse, Morley was in fine spirits. When the band came out on the stage, he yelled and put his hands in the air.

"Come on, everybody. Help me out." He began a slow clap, "ten, nine, eight…" The audience joined in and began counting down with him. When they reached zero, Uncle Teddy struck a tremendous chord on the guitar that reverberated around the room, and Grommet hammered an opening drum solo and then lit into *Cocaine*. The crowd went crazy, hooting and whistling and then burst into motion, rocking and jiving with the rhythm.

Catlyn watched Morley wind up the crowd, leaping to the microphone to holler and growl into it like a man possessed. His energy filled the room, and every eye was on him. His body gyrated with the beat, and sometimes unable to restrain himself, he burst into a sexy dance, his hips thrusting back and forth. By the second set, his T-shirt was drenched and outlined every curve of his arms and chest. Sweat dampened his hair which turned darker around his face while his golden curls shook as he sang. His lips curled around the words, and his teeth shone when he threw his head back and wailed.

Catlyn too moved behind her microphone; unable to keep her feet still, she was drawn into the music's throbbing beat. Rays of light beamed through her eyelashes, decorating the scene before her with a frame of glassy globes. The crowd formed an undulating mass—faces, arms, and legs gesticulating this way and that—pulsing without order but rhythmically, a throbbing squish of flesh, grinding against itself. Catlyn felt the heat of the stage lights, sticking her shirt to her skin. By the third set, she too was wet, and her hair stuck to her neck. She was drained by the relentless push of too much stimulation, too much energy, and just too much. And at the root of it was Morley. As the band rode to its final crescendo, he jumped across the stage, his pumping arm counting down the last beats, until he arrived at the microphone, fist raised high in triumph, as the final shriek from the guitar fell away.

"Thank you!" he called into the microphone. As if planned, a huge roar went up from the roadhouse girls who had formed a thick knot over by the bar.

"Morley! Morley!" they screamed and waved their hands in the air. Morley beamed a huge grin their way. "Why, thank you, ladies," he said with an Elvis rumble. "Thank you very much." The "ladies" went nuts. "Morley! Morley!" They didn't stop chanting until the band was backstage. Morley turned to Catlyn.

"Get the feeling they liked me," he said, pleased.

The next day at rehearsal, the band was a little flat. It had been an exciting couple weeks with a lot of new material, and the night before had taken it out of everyone. Everyone that is except Morley who didn't cut anybody any slack. He re-started the band twice to get the kickoff right and corrected Catlyn three times on her harmonizing. She was relieved to see Sherice show up in the garage, signaling the end of rehearsal.

"Hey, great!" Morley said when he saw her. "We going out to the lake?"

"Only if you're ready to party, babe," said Sherice.

"I sure am—" Morley started, but Catlyn interrupted.

"No," she said. She'd had enough of it: the crowd, the ladies, now Sherice, *enough*.

Morley misunderstood and cocked his head. "Where are we going?" he asked.

"Nowhere!" Catlyn said fiercely. Uncle Teddy's head came up from his guitar, and he looked at her. "You're not coming with us," she snapped at Morley. His head jerked back as though she had slapped him.

"Hey," he said, hurt. Then he too reacted in anger. "Hey, what happened to *Stand By Your Man*?" he said, partly joking and partly not.

For some reason, this made Catlyn even madder.

"Why?" she shouted. "You planning on cheating on me?"

"Not till now," he yelled back.

"Well, you're not coming!" she exploded. "You're—you're not *from here*."

And, with that, past Sherice's shocked face and the rest of the band, she slammed out of the garage and climbed into Danny's truck.

"What's going on?" Danny asked, just as Sherice climbed in and said, "Jesus, Cate, what the hell."

"Shut up!" said Catlyn. "Shut up, everybody." She was close to tears.

"Damn," said Danny, and he and Sherice looked at each other.

"Did he—" Sherice started.

"I don't want to talk about it," said Catlyn hotly.

They did go out to the lake because that was the plan, but of course Catlyn had a terrible time and couldn't stop feeling equally furious at Morley—though she didn't know exactly why—and equally shocked at her own behavior. Danny and Sherice gave her a wide berth and told others to leave her alone. She took off her shoes and waded in the warm lake water until she felt better. She knelt on her heels in the sand and listened to the faraway radio playing *Rocket Man*. By the time Sherice came to get her, she wished she was a rocket man and was high as hell. On the way home, she started to cry.

"What, baby, what?" said Sherice. "Did he do something to you?"

"No, it's me," sobbed Catlyn. "I don't know what's gotten into me."

"This just isn't like you," insisted Sherice.

"Leave her alone," said Danny. "Just leave her the hell alone." For once, Catlyn was grateful to him. She asked them to drop her at the farm instead of going back to Uncle Teddy's. She didn't want to have to face him after what she had done. Her parents were surprised to see her but said nothing when she went straight to her room and shut the door.

Sherice texted her later: *u ok?* Catlyn thought for a while before she responded with: *yeah*

How do you say that you're not okay but there's nothing wrong with you? She pulled out one of her notebooks and puzzled over some lines until she felt sleepy enough to turn out the light. In the dark, she stared at the ceiling and thought about Morley and how this summer had turned out different from any other in her life.

Catlyn kept her head down and just focused on her work at the Cuppa and the farm over the next few days. Sherice watched her carefully but held her tongue. Catlyn heard nothing from Morley which she was thankful for. How she would ever face him again, she had no idea. She tried not to think about it.

On Thursday, she knew she had to show up for rehearsal no matter how much she dreaded it. She crept through the mudroom and peeked in the garage. Morley wasn't there, and the band was unusually quiet. Uncle Teddy turned when she came in.

"Good evening," he said soberly.

"Hi, Uncle Teddy," she said. She felt like she was about seven years old.

"Morley's out of town," he told her. For a moment, she panicked. Had he left because of her?

"He has some family issues to take care of," Uncle Teddy continued, as though reading her mind.

"Family issues!" Catlyn stared at him.

"Cate…" Uncle Teddy paused and looked at her kindly. "Sometimes—sometimes a man could use a little help." She stared at him. She had no idea what he meant.

"You could do that for Morley," he added. Rehearsal was brief and subdued without Morley's bouncing presence and constant interjections. That night, in her room at Uncle Teddy's, Catlyn pulled out her phone and pulled Morley up in her contacts. Her fingers hovered over the screen. She stared at it for a long time and then sighed and put the phone away.

The next morning at the Cuppa, she told Sherice that Morley was gone and what Uncle Teddy had said. Sherice stared at her.

"What do you think that means?" she asked.

"I have no idea," said Catlyn. They speculated briefly, and then Sherice announced, "You should text him."

"I started to, but…" Catlyn began.

"Text him right now," ordered Sherice.

"I'll do it later," Catlyn said.

"Promise?" said Sherice. "I'm gonna check that you did, you know."

"Okay, I promise," said Catlyn.

At home, her parents were quiet at dinner.

"You okay, honey?" asked her mother.

"Fine," said Catlyn, and to her embarrassment, she felt tears start to well up. Her mother and father exchanged a look but didn't say anything more.

Back in her bedroom, she pulled out her phone again. Her fingers hovered over the little screen again. Finally she texted: *u ok?* and quickly put her phone under her pillow. It buzzed a few minutes later. It was from Morley.

hey kitty cat clawed anybody lately? She had to smile. Then he wrote: *had 2 move my mom*

She thought for a long time before she sent her next text. She thought about what Uncle Teddy had said, the night at the Cuppa, and when Morley had come for supper. Mostly she thought about Morley.

Finally, she wrote: *do u want me 2 come?* His response was immediate: *yes but u can do it there* She blushed. She didn't know what to say. After a pause, he texted: *miss u* She wrote back: *me 2* And she did.

Sherice texted later: *did u do it*

yes Catlyn typed.

u guys make up

yes

i knew it

Uncle Teddy came for dinner on Saturday since it was the Pitchforks' night off from The Corral. Now Catlyn was looking forward to seeing him although he was discreet enough to say nothing in front of her parents. After the dishes were cleared and they were alone in the dining room, he told her that rehearsals were cancelled until Morley was back and asked if she had been in touch.

"I texted him," she said.

"You kids," said Uncle Teddy. "Why don't you just call him?"

"Maybe I will," she said. "Do you know what's going on with his mom?"

"She has issues," said Uncle Teddy.

"Like what?" insisted Catlyn.

"I'll let Morley go into that," said Uncle Teddy. Catlyn wanted to ask more, but she held her tongue.

On Thursday, when Catlyn walked into Uncle Teddy's house after leaving the Cuppa, Morley was sitting in the kitchen. Catlyn flew to him and threw herself upon him before he was fully out of his chair.

"Hey, Kitty Cat," he said, startled. "Nice to see you too."

"I can't believe you would just show up!" she said.

"Don't get mad," he said raising his hands in alarm. "I wanted to surprise you."

"Besides," he said delicately, "the last time I saw you, you—I know this is hard to believe—you weren't that happy with me."

"Well," she said, stepping back to check him out. "Did you cheat on me in California?"

"What? No!" he said, alarmed. She looked up and hugged him again.

Just then, Uncle Teddy walked in and pulled a pitcher of iced tea out of the refrigerator.

"Happy now, Cate?" he asked, pouring the tea into glasses.

"Very," said Catlyn. And she didn't care who knew it. Morley beamed. They both took big gulps of tea.

"Mmm," said Morley. Catlyn hid her smirk.

"I have big news," said Uncle Teddy. "Word has gotten around about Morley. A couple of Sony execs from Nashville are coming up to The Corral on Saturday to check him out." Morley and Catlyn stared at him dumbfounded.

"Yeah," he continued. "Some big wig was at the July Fourth concert." Catlyn's stomach hit the floor. Morley had just gotten back, and now this. *You knew this was coming,* she told herself, *you knew this.* It was true; it was just that everything was happening so fast.

CHAPTER ELEVEN

The Pitchforks flew into action. Uncle Teddy's announcement meant that they had two days to get ready for Morley's big gig. The guys re-arranged schedules and showed up at Uncle Teddy's house to hold the Thursday rehearsal as usual. There was considerable discussion about what material they should use. Catlyn was in favor of moving her microphone back to its spot next to the band to leave the spotlight on Morley, but he would have none of it.

"We're doing our show the way we always do it," he said. "I don't care who these guys are. They might not even show." But the news seemed to have given him an excuse to be more persnickety than ever. He went over the set list twice and then started re-grooving the back-up vocals for *Can't Breath*. While he was messing around with the timing on *Diamond Joe*, the guys mostly just stared at him implacable. Uncle Teddy didn't say much—just kept patiently trying things out and providing input. He did say that it was better not to change too much at this point, but that didn't seem to slow Morley down. They got through about half the set list, and then the guys headed home with the agreement that they would finish up the next day. Emotionally burnt out, Catlyn sat down in a chair in the garage while Morley picked at a bass, hummed, and fiddled with one of the amplifiers. She watched him and wondered how he could not be exhausted after the previous week and his trip.

"How's your mom?" she asked finally. He paused and reflected as though he had forgotten he had a mother.

"Well, she's in her new place," he said. He left it at that and went back to futzing around.

"Ready to go?" he said, after a time.

"I don't know…" Catlyn said. It was almost nine-thirty, and she was scheduled to work at the Cuppa the next day. Morley looked distressed, and he moved to her.

"Please come, Cat," he said urgently. He put his arms around her. Catlyn remembered her uncle's words.

"Of course, I'll come," she corrected herself. Morley gave her a big kiss and swatted her on the butt.

"Atta girl," he said. He seemed genuinely relieved.

In bed that night, Morley got his needs met, but he was considerate and passionate, taking his time with her until she too climaxed and rocked with him. She fought back tears after they were both still.

"Morley, I—" she said. Her voice shook.

"Hey, shhh, shhh," he said, moving to gather her in his arms. "That's enough."

"I feel terrible. I just got so mad—I don't even know—"

"Stop," he said. "We are not like that. We will not be like that. We are not rattled by dumb shit. Okay? That's not us." He kissed her on the forehead and squeezed her shoulders.

"Okay," she said tearily. She hoped he was right. He seemed so convinced. He wasn't like any boyfriend she'd ever had before, that was for sure.

The next morning, he walked Catlyn to the Cuppa, ostensibly to check on the new oven.

"It's working great!" Sherice said. "Here, try for yourself." Morley taste-tested a muffin and declared the oven the best in the country. He kissed Catlyn goodbye in front of Sherice and the customers, making her turn pink.

"I knew you guys would make up," said Sherice.

Catlyn called home to tell her mother that she wouldn't be home for chores until after rehearsal.

"Is Morley back?" asked her mother carefully.

"Yeah," said Catlyn.

"How are things?" Catlyn felt a lump in her throat.

"Mom, I—"

"Aw, honey," said Marie. The kindness in her mother's voice brought Catlyn even closer to tears. "Here's the thing," Marie continued. "Love is a bunch of emotions all rolled up into one. Sometimes things that don't look like love really are love."

Like harmonics, Catlyn thought. *You have to listen for the sweetness.* "You mean, like strip away the distractions," she said.

"That sounds right. I'm no expert. But your dad and I try to keep things simple," said Marie. "Because love is messy."

"Thanks, Mom," said Catlyn.

"Hey, we were thinking of coming to The Corral tomorrow. Will it be a good show?"

Catlyn told her mother about the Sony executives. Her mother was quiet for a while.

"It's hard to know what that means," she said finally. "One thing at a time, okay?"

Morley might have been talking a good game about keeping the songs the same, but his level of tension kept rising as Friday's rehearsal wore on. Catlyn tried to keep up with his instructions on the harmony parts, but they were too complicated and she was making mistakes. At one point, he whirled on her.

"Count, Cat!" he snarled. "You gotta count. You know how to count, don't you?" Catlyn felt the ground fall out from under her. She stared at him and blinked, speechless.

"And you," he turned to Grommet. "I could go for coffee, waiting for you to pick up the beat. You—" But that was all he got out.

"Stop," said Uncle Teddy, and that one word served as the final warning.

"Fuck!" said Morley and slammed out of the room. Catlyn stood there with her mouth open. She looked at Uncle Teddy in shock.

"He's just nervous about tomorrow," he said. "Nothing to worry about."

But Catlyn had had enough. She followed Morley and called after him, "Hey! Loudmouth!" He paused, his back rigid, and then she saw him relax and let the tension go. He turned toward her with a sheepish grin.

"Cat," he said. "Sorry about being an asshole."

"Funny, I had that happen to me… once," she said. He smiled and took her hand.

They walked for a few minutes.

"Tomorrow is really important," he said.

"Why?" she asked. "Why is it?"

"Because—" He sighed and then said in a rush, "Because your uncle set it up for me, and they have expectations."

"Okay," she said slowly, processing this. "What do you mean, Uncle Teddy set it up?"

"Cat," said Morley, "you don't know this, but your uncle is pretty well-known in the business. It's not just that he's talented. People respect him. He's given me a chance—"

Something clicked in Catlyn's mind. It didn't surprise her that Uncle Teddy had noticed Morley. He was remarkable. But, for the first time, it occurred to her that Uncle Teddy hadn't brought Morley here for the band—he had done it for Morley.

"Your uncle really helped me," said Morley. "More than you know. Things were bad in Austin. I didn't have a gig; I was couch-surfing. He knows my mother, and he found me. And he gave me a place here. An opportunity."

Couch-surfing He knows my mother An opportunity. Catlyn tried to process all this information. She was dying to ask questions. *Wait*, she thought, *wait.*

"The band will be great," she finally said. "Don't worry. Just get your own shit together."

He wrapped his arms around her and looked down into her face. He rubbed her cheekbone with his thumb.

"Thanks. Who says dogs are a man's best friend," he said and kissed her lightly on the mouth.

That evening, Catlyn sat on the porch after feeding the animals. Robert's black cowboy hat was sitting next to her on the swing, and she picked it up and turned it over in her hands. It was worn in places, but the silver trim still shone in the semi-darkness. Her dad had had it as long as she could remember, and she thought about where all the hat had been and how much it had seen. A hat like that would know things, she observed, and her thoughts moved on to Morley's outburst.

The thing was she didn't always count the beats the way she should; she did just depend on him to count her in, and the reality was that she wasn't as dedicated or professional or talented as he was. She loved music, no doubt, but, as a singer, he was operating on a different level. She thought about Morley going around singing songs in his head and Uncle Teddy giving Morley an opportunity. An *opportunité*, she thought. *That makes two of us.*

If Morley had been showing a case of nerves on Friday, they vanished on Saturday night. It was the first time the Pitchforks had played at The Corral since the July Fourth concert, and word had obviously spread about the hot band from Upton. The sprawling parking lot was already nearly full when the band arrived to set up their equipment. Morley and Uncle Teddy were keyed up, and their elation spread to the rest of the band. The place was already rocking thirty minutes into the first set, and Morley was on fire, winding the crowd up and then setting the girls to screaming when he stormed around the stage and manhandled the microphone. Some of the girls at the bar seemed close to hysterics when he sang *The Fireman*. The band was playing out of their mind. Catlyn had never heard them so tight, and loud, and *on it*. She knew they were killing it, and her heart swelled with pride and joy to be able to show off her beautiful boy to those Nashville guys. When she sang *Can't Even Get the Blues*, Uncle Teddy's guitar wailed behind her, and Morley got the crowd to join in on the chorus. At the break, the band tumbled backstage, wound up and full of adrenalin. Morley whooped and was snapping a towel at Grommet.

"That sounded great!" he told the band. He grabbed Catlyn, gave her a smooch, and waltzed her around in the small space. "We are *all* hot tonight, boys!" he crowed.

Donelle appeared at the door and ushered two men into the back room. Uncle Teddy went over to shake hands and then introduced them to the band. They shook hands with each of the band members, including Catlyn. She was so distracted that she missed their names entirely. *I guess this shaking hands stuff is what out-of-towners do,* she said to herself, remembering Morley shaking her hand when they first met. The men were casually dressed, but it was clear from their expensive boots and haircuts that they weren't local. They gathered around a little standup table with Morley and Uncle Teddy. The rest of the band busied themselves with their phones or instruments or drinks. After a few minutes, Morley called Catlyn to join them at the little table.

"Here's my secret weapon," he said. "She's what makes me sound good." He took her hand under the table.

"Yeah, awesome chemistry," one of the execs said, and Catlyn knew in that instant that they didn't have the slightest interest in her. They only had eyes for Morley. She wasn't surprised. Singers like her were probably a dime a dozen in Nashville. She also discovered that she didn't care. It was Morley's night, and she wanted him to knock those guys out.

Rumors flew the rest of the night that the execs had left, that they were still there, that they had come back, but Morley was unfazed by all of it. He put on a fabulous show, and the crowd went crazy for it. They danced their hearts out to *Faster Car*, cackled when Morley and Catlyn sang *Jackson*, and wolf-whistled when Morley spun her around the stage to *Why Don't We Just Dance*. Catlyn saw her parents two-stepping to *Born to Fly*. She watched Morley entertaining the crowd, wooing and wowing them, and thought to herself, *Check him out, boys. You got anything like in Nashville? Bet you don't.* But she tried not to think too much about Nashville. After the band was finished playing, Catlyn's parents came backstage to say hi, despite the late hour.

"Congratulations," Robert said to Morley, tipping his hat. "That was a helluva good time, son."

"Hey, I appreciate you folks coming out," Morley said. "And thanks for telling me how to use the hat." He tipped his own back at Robert. They all laughed.

"Gotta favor to ask you," Robert continued. "Gotta move a steer tomorrow. Think you could come out and help me?" Catlyn stared at her dad, who had never asked any of her friends for help before, then turned to look at Morley to see how he would react to this request.

"Thought you'd never ask," said Morley. "Just… what is a steer?"

 CHAPTER TWELVE

Morley showed in the morning the next day, dressed for work in jeans and a T-shirt. Robert loaned him a pair of boots.

"Don't want you getting stepped on in—whatever those are," he gestured at Morley's sneakers.

Morley seemed genuinely pleased to put in some hard labor at the farm. Catlyn worried his typical brashness might get him in trouble, but he listened carefully to Robert and had good intuition about how things worked. He was strong, too, maybe stronger than Robert, although Catlyn thought she wouldn't want to bet on him in a fight. *He'd start laughing in the middle,* she thought. Robert got him up on the tractor which they both got a huge kick out of.

"This is just like *Farmer's Daughter*!" he called to Catlyn when he encountered her in the barn. When they got around to loading the steer, Robert positioned himself at the front of the trailer to pull on a rope attached to the steer's halter. He put Morley and Catlyn behind the steer to encourage him to climb in. The steer, of course, had other ideas. They pushed and cajoled, but he would have none of it. They passed a rope around his backside to encourage him, but he just leaned back against the rope and snorted, tossing his head. After swatting the steer, slapping him on the rear, and tugging on the rope, all to no avail, Morley finally lost patience with him, leaned into his side, grabbed him around the front legs, lifted him partially up on his shoulder and shoved him into the trailer.

"There," Morley said while Catlyn and her dad looked at him. "Kinda like a really big dumb bell."

"All right then," said Robert and gave Catlyn a grin. The steer stood in the trailer, looking surprised.

Band rehearsal had been cancelled that night to give everyone a night off after their big Saturday night triumph. Morley stayed for dinner and dug into Marie's feast of pork chops, macaroni and cheese, and canned peaches.

"I'd work all day any day for a dinner like this," he said, when he finally stopped eating. "Just text me, and I'll come running," he told Robert.

"*Text* you?" said Robert and arched his eyebrows.

"Ah… just tell Catlyn," Morley re-phrased.

Marie shooed Morley and Catlyn out the door for a walk before it got too dark. They headed up in the direction of the barn. It was still warm, and the lightning bugs were out. Catlyn could hear the chickens clucking quietly in their roost. Morley took her hand as they strolled. They were both quiet for a while.

"When do you think you might hear anything from Nashville?" she finally couldn't resist asking.

"Already did," he said and swung her hand a little. "They called earlier." She turned and stared at him.

"They did? What did they say?" she said.

"They want me to come down to Nashville," he said. "They say they can set some things up for me—some gigs and introduce me around, do some recording."

"Are they going to sign you?" she asked.

"I guess that's the general idea," he said.

"Well, that's fantastic, Morley," she said, and in that moment, she didn't think about her feelings or what that meant for her. She was truly happy for him.

"The thing is…" Morley paused and took her other hand. "I—" He stopped. "Can we sit down somewhere?" he said.

"Of course." She peered at him with concern. Once they were seated on the feed box in the barn, he took her hand again. He looked in her face, and Catlyn realized how emotional he was.

"What, Morley, what's wrong?"

"I—" He caught himself again and then straightened his back with resolve.

"I can't go without you," he said suddenly.

"Excuse me?" Catlyn couldn't hide her amazement.

"I know I can't really ask you to leave all this." He gestured around at the barn and the deepening gloom and the farm. "Your family, and… But, Cat, you just *have* to come with me." He took her hand in both of his. Catlyn blinked and looked down at her lap. It had never occurred to her that Morley would ask her to go with him. It was simply inconceivable.

"I know this is a shock," he continued. "But, you know, if you're serious about songwriting—" Catlyn raised her head in surprise and stared at him. "I've seen your notebooks," he said and smiled a little. "If you're serious about that, there are people in Nashville who can help you, who can teach you. And—" he continued, looking into her face, "if you did want to go to college—"

Catlyn blinked again. There had been talk of college when she first graduated high school. She had been a good student, and her teachers had encouraged her to apply. She and her parents had talked about it a little—until they didn't talk about it anymore. *College!* Catlyn stared at Morley.

"They have good schools there," he was saying. "So, there would be opportunity for you there." *There's that word again*, thought Catlyn.

"But I'm not going to pretend this is for you," Morley said. "Believe me, I recognize what I would be taking you away from. But, I need you, Cat. I need you more than I've ever needed anything. I *have* to have you there."

Catlyn stared at him. Was this the same cocky Morley they all knew and loved? She had never seen him so serious in her life.

"I've been alone way too much in my life," he said. "I can't keep on being so damned alone all the time. And now I've finally got the woman I want to spend the rest of my life with, and this thing has come up in Nashville…"

Catlyn's brain seemed to have gone into slow motion: *alone too much, rest of life, this thing.* Morley was still talking.

"…marry me. Please say yes, Cat…" Things had slowed down so much that Catlyn decided she must be dreaming. She looked at this beautiful boy. *Such a nice dream*, she thought, *about a dreamy guy*. She admired his long lashes over those golden eyes. *A brown-eyed boy*.

"Cat?" Morley was peering at her. She sighed happily and smiled at him.

"Are you okay?" he said. He looked at her anxiously. "You're not going to freak out on me, are you?" It dawned on her that this dream was turning strange.

"Ah… did you say 'marry?'" she asked him, feeling ridiculous.

"Yes," he said. "Getting married—that's what I'm talking about. I wouldn't ask you to go down there without some kind of commitment. Please, Cat, would you think about it?"

"Are you asking me to marry you?" she finally burst out, the realization crashing down on her, like a bucket of cold water.

"I'm doing a shitty job of it," he said, "but, yeah, Cat, that's what I'm driving at. I love you. I want us to be together." He drew her to him. Catlyn shook her head slowly to clear her mind.

"Don't shake your head," he said. "I think this is a good idea. Okay, let me put it this way: why *wouldn't* you marry me?" Catlyn began to sense that the old Morley was coming back. She wasn't sure she was happy about that, but she smiled ruefully. He smiled too, hooked a finger under her chin, and kissed her.

"Come on," he whispered. But Catlyn rose to the challenge.

"I don't know how you do these things where you come from, Mr. California," she said, "but out here, we don't marry each other that fast." Morley took a breath and squeezed her hand, relieved to have her speak.

"I thought you might say that," he said. "But here's the thing: we've actually spent a lot of time together this summer. And I feel like I know you—although you're hard to keep up with sometimes. And I *know* you know me. Besides, who has a stopwatch on falling in love?"

Oh my, she thought, *there's a line.* But she wasn't finished.

"What if we don't make it?" she said uneasily. "A lot of couples don't."

"Two things," he said urgently. He seemed ready with a lot of answers, she noticed. "We'll make it if we decide to make it. If we don't get distracted by the wrong things, I know we can do it. Because that's how we are," he said with determination. *Harmonics,* thought Catlyn. *That's what Mom said.*

Morley was continuing. "And, two, since when have you turned into a scaredy-cat?" She looked at him. *Never,* she thought. *I'm not a scaredy-cat.* She said nothing more. He grinned.

"All right! You love me, right, Cat?" he urged. Then, "Wait, don't answer that. Because—I love you, okay?" She still said nothing, but couldn't resist smiling at him. *Do I love him?* she thought. And almost immediately, *Absolutely, he fills me with joy, makes me laugh… and other things.* Morley was talking again.

"I don't have a ring for you," he was saying. "I didn't know where to get one here, and I thought you might want to pick out your own anyway…" She put a finger on his lips.

"I haven't said yes, yet," she said, and Morley looked aghast.

"But you will, right, Cat?"

"I have to think about it," she told him.

"Okay, I know, but… well, just make sure you say yes."

They walked back to his truck, and he filled her in on the details of what the Nashville guys had said. It was hard to think about all the things that were about to change. Morley kissed her again, deeply this time, and pressed himself against her. She felt the warmth of his body, and a small flame of desire lit inside her.

"We are going to be so good together," he whispered. "You'll see."

After Morley left and she walked back in the house, her parents were sitting in the living room. That was unusual, but Catlyn was so thunderstruck she joined them without wondering what they were doing there.

"He asked me to marry him," she said. She almost couldn't believe the words coming out of her mouth. Her parents looked at her but didn't seem surprised. Robert cleared his throat.

"He asked me about that." Catlyn felt her back go up.

"What do you mean?"

"He said he didn't know how things were done around here, but that he wanted to propose to you. He said he'd feel better if I said it was okay. I didn't know guys did that anymore." Robert sounded a little pleased. Catlyn thought that using Morley as an example for how guys did things was probably a dangerous practice.

"What did you say," she demanded.

"I said it was your decision." They looked at each other. Catlyn thought about Morley asking Robert for his daughter's hand in marriage. It struck her as funny, and she couldn't help tittering. Her parents joined in.

"He must think we're from the last century," said Marie. Eventually, Robert asked, "What did you tell the boy?"

"I didn't," said Catlyn. "I told him I'd have to think about it."

"Smart," said Robert.

"He was worried he didn't have a ring," said Marie. Catlyn was amazed. *Some guy from California I've known for three months is asking me to marry him, and all everyone is worried about is a ring*, she thought. Then it occurred to her that three months ago, she might have been more worried about a ring too. Things had changed.

"He talked about you guys moving to Nashville," said her father. Catlyn couldn't believe those words were coming out of her dad's mouth either. "You could talk to Uncle Teddy about that." Catlyn knew right away that was a good suggestion. Now, though, she wanted time to be by herself and think about how her life had been turned upside down in one summer and turned into a Tilt-a-Whirl in one day.

She tossed and turned during the night. Her thoughts roamed from being a country music star's wife and living a tacky life of riches and parties to turning into an old hag on her parents' farm, impoverished and alone. She dreamed that she was roaming city streets, lost and bewildered. "Don't be a scaredy-cat," a passerby whispered. It was a relief when dawn came. Her phone rang at six. It was Morley.

"You awake?" he said low into the phone, and his voice sent a thrill through her.

"Yes," she said. "Barely."

"Didn't sleep much," he said. She wasn't sure if he meant her or him, but either way, she suspected it was true. She thought of him in his airless basement, staring at the ceiling or pacing the concrete floor, and she wished she could put her arms around him. The sound of his voice cheered her, and her spirits rose. It looked like a beautiful day, they had their whole lives ahead of them, and for now, they had each other.

"Morley?" she said.

"Um-hum." He tried to sound cool, but she could hear him breathing into the phone.

"Thanks for yesterday," she said. "For everything."

Morley chuckled, and it all seemed so much better.

"You're welcome, Kit Kat. I hope that steer stays put wherever he is now, and—lucky for you—the marriage proposal still stands. Just don't keep me waiting too long." She laughed then too. They made arrangements to see each other at the farm later.

Catlyn then called Uncle Teddy and asked if he had time to talk that day. He didn't seem surprised to hear from her. Robert needed to get some supplies at the feed store, and he dropped her at Uncle Teddy's for a chat.

"Hello, kiddo," said Uncle Teddy. "No iced tea today. I'm out of mix."

"That's okay," said Catlyn quickly. Uncle Teddy gave her a knowing look.

"Now, I've been talking to Morley about the business side of what he could be getting himself into," he said. "But moving to that town and getting married and all that, that's a whole different kettle of fish." Catlyn nodded.

"You know I only want the best for you," said Uncle Teddy. He hesitated, and she thought she could see a mist in his eyes. *Dear Uncle Teddy*, she thought.

"But here's how I see it. I can't tell you if you should marry Morley or not; that's a matter for your heart and head to decide. But I do know Nashville. It's not an easy town. It's big and political and full of broken hearts. The music business is fickle, and innocent people get hurt. But I'd feel a whole hell of a lot better about sending you or Morley down there if the two of you went together. That's a combination that just might work."

"Were you in Nashville, Uncle Teddy?"

"I was. I had dreams, and I probably could have eked out a living. I would never have been a star—the industry wants beautiful people for that, and, in case you haven't noticed, I'm not going to win any beauty contests." Catlyn chortled.

"You look good to me," she said.

"You better get those pretty eyes checked."

A minute later, she asked, "How did you know Morley's mom?" Uncle Teddy paused.

"Let's just say she was in the entertainment business too."

"I know Morley really appreciates what you did for him."

"That boy has a lot of potential. But he needs support, Cate. He doesn't have a family, like you, or much of one. You two would have to look out for each other. I'll do what I can from here, but Nashville can be a hard place. I told Morley I'd act as his manager until he gets a real one, but you guys have to deal with the day-to-day. And don't forget that you have options. There's no shame in coming home."

"I can't imagine Morley doing anything other than singing."

"You never know. I hear he might have a future in steer wrangling." They both laughed. "Seriously, though, you have to remember your options. The ones who get hurt are the ones who think there's nothing else they can do."

"Thanks, Uncle Teddy. That's really helpful."

———

"You're a remarkable person, Cate. You have your wits about you, and you have more talent than you realize. You and Morley could be very successful down there. But you have to take care of each other."

"We will," promised Catlyn. "Also, Uncle Teddy? Remember what you said when Morley first came here?"

"I do."

"Well, I appreciate the opportunité." He laughed and patted her on the shoulder.

"It turned into more of an opportunité than I knew at the time, my girl. And maybe this opportunité in Nashville will turn out to be just as good."

Later, at the farm, Catlyn took Morley out onto the porch and told him about her conversation with Uncle Teddy. He watched her face and eyes and waited, his chest barely rising and falling.

"I think you should go," she said to him. "It's a chance of a lifetime for you." He started to speak, but she put a finger against his lips.

"You know how you mentioned this thing about getting married last night?" she asked.

His lips barely moved. "Did I? Must have slipped my mind."

"I have an answer."

"I better like this."

"I thought you'd never ask."

Morley whooped and fist-pumped the air. "That means yes, right?" he said, and without waiting for an answer, he jumped up from the swing and danced around the porch with Catlyn. They heard stirring from inside the house. Morley yanked open the front door and danced her inside.

"She said yes!" he yelled toward the kitchen. Marie appeared in the doorway.

"Oh my goodness," she said, a smile on her face despite the tears in her eyes. Robert came out of his office and shook Morley's hand.

"Congratulations, son," he said. "You're a brave man." He winked at Catlyn.

"Hey!" she said. "I'm braver."

"You're both brave," said Marie. "Let's celebrate! I've got some ice cream in the freezer."

Late that night, after lots of conversation and planning, the hubbub finally died down, and Morley headed home. Catlyn sat on the porch and looked out at the farm that meant so much to her and thought about the life ahead, full of unknowns and new adventures, but with a man she loved and trusted. As she thought about what she would encounter and what she was leaving, a verse came to her:

Home always has to stay behind

It never gets to go

No matter what else you find

Home stays home

PLAYLISTS

Playlist for the Rusty Pitchforks   Artist/Songwriter

First Set:

American Saturday Night	Brad Paisley
Sunshine & Whiskey	Frankie Ballard
Joe's Place	Joe Nichols
Room to Breath	Chase Bryant
You've Got to Stand for Something	Charley Pride
Pink Houses	John Cougar Mellencamp
Rollin' With the Flow	Charlie Rich
I Feel Lucky	Mary Chapin Carpenter
Diamond Joe	Traditional
The Fireman	George Strait
Prayin' for Daylight	Rascal Flatts
Walking the Dog	Rufus Thomas
Giddy Up and Go	Teddy Lagrange

Second Set:

That's the Way I Feel	Delbert McClinton
Samson & Delilah	Traditional/Grateful Dead
Why Don't We Just Dance	Josh Turner

Your Cheatin' Heart	Hank Williams
Some Days You Gotta Dance	Dixie Chicks
Heart on a String	Jason Isbell and the 400 Unit
Under Your Spell Again	Buck Owens
New Chick in the Henhouse	Teddy Lagrange
Drinkin' Problem	Midland
Heard It Through the Grapevine	Gladys Knight & the Pips
Neon Moon	Brooks & Dunn
Born to Fly	Sara Evans
Honky Tonkin'	Hank Williams

Third Set:

Faster Car	Keith Urban
Folsom Prison Blues	Johnny Cash
Good Ol' Boy (Gettin' Tough)	Steve Earle and the Dukes
Cocaine	J.J. Cale/ Eric Clapton
Lovin' All Night	Rodney Crowell
Fast as You	Dwight Yoakam
The Pirate's Supper	Teddy Lagrange
Silver Thunderbird	Marc Cohn
Little Sister	Elvis Presley
Georgia On My Mind	Hoagy Carmichael/Ray Charles
Last Base	Teddy Lagrange
Workin' Man's Blues	Merle Haggard
Home Sweet Home	The Farm

Special for the July Fourth Concert or Alternatives:

Better Find a Church	JD and the Straight Shot
It's Different for Girls	Dierks Bentley (Feat. Elle King)
Jackson	Johnny Cash and June Carter
Can't Even Get the Blues	Reba McEntire

Blue Ain't Your Color	Keith Urban
You Are So Beautiful	Billy Preston/Joe Cocker
This Boy's Kin	Corinne Arbeau

Playlist for Catlyn's Benefit Concert:

Joe's Place	Joe Nichols
Don't Think Twice	Bob Dylan
Gentle on My Mind	John Hartford/Glen Campbell
Carey	Joni Mitchell
The Boxer	Simon and Garfunkel
Letter to Me	Brad Paisley
The Lucky One	Alison Krauss and Union Station
You've Got a Friend	Carole King
Time After Time	Cyndi Lauper
American Pie	Don McLean
Let It Be	The Beatles

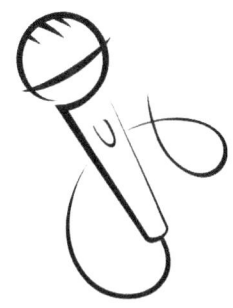

About the Author

Corinne Arbeau grew up in the rural Midwest and spent much of her childhood reading, in between chores. She now lives in California with her family and splits her time between the mountains and the ocean. She still spends time reading, in between chores, and savors a good love story. A lifelong music fan, she's always on the lookout for an exceptional song.

www.ingramcontent.com/pod-product-compliance
Lightning Source LLC
Chambersburg PA
CBHW071321130626
46556CB00004B/1689